Falling for His
Best Friend

an Out of Uniform novel

Katee Robert

Entangled Publishing, LLC
2614 South Timberline Road
Suite 109
Fort Collins, CO 80525
Visit our website at www.entangledpublishing.com.

Brazen is an imprint of Entangled Publishing, LLC. For more information on our titles, visit www.brazenbooks.com.

Edited by Heather Howland
Cover design by Heather Howland
Cover art by Shutterstock

Manufactured in the United States of America

First Edition May 2015

To my babies. Yes, you'll always be my babies, even when you're forty-five. I love you so much!

Chapter One

Drew Flannery was so goddamn late. He was supposed to meet his best friend, Avery, at Chilly's forty minutes ago. She'd mentioned something about exciting news and now he was fucking up what he expected was her well-planned out delivery.

He ducked into his police cruiser and cursed. The whole thing reeked of alcohol and stale cigarettes, an unnecessary reminder of *why* he was late. The town drunk, Rusty, had decided today would be a good day to lose his shit and cause a scene at the liquor store. He'd shattered four six-packs before Drew was able to hustle him out, and everyone knew he wouldn't pay for the damage.

Which was why Drew found himself slipping Mr. Christianson two twenties to make up for it.

He threw the cruiser into gear and pulled out of the sheriff department's parking lot. As annoying as he found dealing with Rusty, he had even less tolerance than normal today. This wasn't the first time he'd slipped Mr. Christianson cash for damages. Hell, the first time he'd done it, he'd been fifteen. The money should have gone to feeding his little brother, Ryan, but he'd felt so guilty and embarrassed when his old man knocked over a display of vodka, he'd given it all up.

Christ, he hadn't thought of that in years.

Drew flew home, breaking more than one traffic law as he did, but it was a necessary evil. After the day he'd had, he needed a drink like nobody's business, and that wasn't something he could swing while in his uniform—or his cruiser. *Going to be even later, but… Hell.* Avery would understand. He hoped.

Thirty minutes later, he rushed into the parking lot in front of Chilly's. In light of how he'd spent the end of his shift, the bar didn't look as welcoming as it usually did. He'd picked Rusty up from here one too many times, called by one waitress or another, who didn't want to deal with a misbehaving drunk. If Avery wasn't inside, he would have turned around and gone home.

Hell, who was he kidding? He would have gone to her place.

Nothing helped him deal with this kind of shit like spending a few hours with Avery. She'd hand him a beer, make a joke, and brighten his day—a routine they'd started almost twenty years ago. Although back then, the way they'd dealt with the hard parts of life was to sneak off together and get into mischief.

He rubbed a hand over his face. He needed to shake this mood. When they'd talked earlier, she'd sounded kind of strange. Whatever this "exciting" news was, it was obviously important if she refused to spill it over the phone. The last thing she needed was for him to walk in like a ticking time bomb, wound up tight over memories.

The thought got him out of the car and moving to the faded blue door at the entrance. Inside, it was dim and smelled faintly of greasy bar food and a combination of oak and beer, something he'd always identified with Chilly's. The low twanging country music meant Gena was on shift. She loved old school Garth Brooks.

He rounded the corner and caught sight of *her*. Though he recognized that his brother and sister-in-law—and his new niece—were also at the table, all he saw was his best friend. It was always like this—a full three seconds of drinking her in, from the carelessly graceful way she carried herself to the long dark hair that he couldn't help tugging on whenever he had the chance.

Which was right about when reality kicked him in the face and reminded him that this was *Avery*, his partner in crime. The one woman on this planet he had no business thinking those kinds of thoughts about.

Even knowing that, just being in the same room as she was loosened something in his chest. He stepped forward, the last hour slipping away, but froze when she turned to say something to Bri and he caught the expression on her face.

She looked…nervous. Almost scared.

The feel-good moment disappeared in a puff of smoke. She'd needed him, and he'd been off dealing with a drunk.

The story of his goddamn life.

Rationally, he knew he needed a few minutes to get his head on straight, but he cut through the tables to where they sat anyway. "Hey."

If anything, she looked even more nervous at the sight of him. What the hell kind of news was she about to drop on him?

Avery dredged up a smile that didn't look a thing like her normal bright grin. "Hey."

"You're late."

He turned to his brother, grateful for the reprieve from the strange awkwardness that had sprung up between him and Avery. "I got a last minute call."

Ryan raised his eyebrows, his dark coloring and blue eyes strikingly similar to Drew's own. "Saving a kitten from a tree again?"

"It's not Thursday." Even the ongoing joke about little six-year-old Kristen's adventurous kitten wasn't enough to shake the reminder of what he *had* been doing. He dropped into the chair next to Avery and raised his hand to get Gena's attention. He needed a goddamn beer. Once she'd motioned to show she'd seen him, he turned back to Avery. "Now, tell me what's going on."

She took a deep breath. "I'm going to have a baby."

• • •

Avery Yeung didn't normally blurt something out and then wish she could take it back, but the shocked silence that descended on the table made her want to do just that. Even baby Lily, the newest addition to the group, stopped her adorable gurgling.

She looked from face to face, her resolve threatening to crumble as the moment stretched on. Even as the thought crossed her mind, she tossed it away. There would be no crumbling and no backing out now that she'd made her choice. It wasn't one she'd made easily, and she wasn't going to back down.

But it would be really nice if someone would say *something*.

She could practically feel Drew's glare boring a hole in the side of her head, but she refused to look at her best friend. Considering his surly entrance a minute ago, she'd expected his reaction to be…less than pleased. But it was her decision to make, damn it, and she was tired of waiting for her "someday." Not when each year brought her closer to the big two-eight.

That particular birthday was like a giant sword hanging over the neck of her family. Her mother had been twenty-eight when she was diagnosed with the cancer that eventually took her life. Her sister, Alexis, had been twenty-eight when she received the same diagnosis. There'd been only one option for her sister—a full hysterectomy and several devastating rounds of treatment. Now that they knew Avery had the same genetic flags, she'd be forced to follow the same path if her body betrayed her. And the odds certainly weren't stacked in her favor.

If she wanted to have her own children, it was now or never.

Her friend, Bri, finally spoke up, "Did you just say you're going to have a baby?"

"Yeah. I don't exactly want to get into the dirty details yet, but I wanted you three to be the first to know." She'd wanted her sister to be there, too, but Alexis deserved to hear this one-on-one.

Drew's brother, Ryan, shook his head as if physically

discarding the shock. "I guess congratulations are in order. Or am I jumping a few steps ahead?"

"Just a few." She'd already been through the screening process at the fertility clinic and picked out the donor, but there were still several steps left before she would be successfully pregnant.

In vitro fertilization. Such a cold name for the fulfillment of the dream she'd had since she was a kid. Granted, in her dream, she hadn't been a *single* mother, but she didn't have a choice. Not with the clock in her head *tick-tick-tick*ing along to a really messed up soundtrack that never let her forget how little time she might have left.

"Congratulations?" Drew dragged his hand through his dark, curly hair. "What the hell are we congratulating her for? You're crazy for doing this, Avery. Fucking nuts."

There it was. The objection she'd *known* he wouldn't be able to hold back for long. Of the two Flannery brothers, Drew had taken his role as protector above and beyond the call of duty. She'd lost count of the guys he'd run off in high school before she'd threatened to knock in his teeth if he didn't stop interfering. She was pretty sure he hadn't stopped—either that or she was such a winner that men had the habit of disappearing after the first couple of dates.

Avery sipped her beer and rotated in her seat to face him, shoring up her courage. She'd really wanted his support—had counted on it, even—but she wasn't going to change her course just because he had a stick shoved up his ass. "It's a good thing I'm not asking your permission, then, isn't it?"

His face went blotchy from anger, and a petty part of her enjoyed the crack in the pretty-boy facade he wore like a badge of honor, the same way he wore his Sheriff's badge.

"Have you even thought about this? Or are you just jumping in head first and hoping for the best?"

Of course she'd thought about it. She'd spent the last two years agonizing over this choice, all while hoping that someone would walk into her life so she wouldn't have to make it alone. But she'd been unwaveringly, depressingly single, aside from a few dates that didn't bear talking about. Drew knew that. He was the one she spent most of her weekends with.

"You know why I'm doing this."

Just like that, his expression changed, some of the anger draining away. "Yeah, I do. But don't you think this is a big step?"

"You mean having a baby isn't a decision to be taken lightly?" She pressed her hand to her chest and gave a mock gasp. "That changes everything."

"Smart ass."

Ryan cleared his throat, bringing their attention back across the table. He nudged Bri, and she practically lit up at the contact. Avery took a moment to grin at the knowledge that she was a big part of the reason they were together. She'd had a gut feeling that her friend and Drew's brother would get along like a house on fire, but even she hadn't seen them getting married and having a baby in just outside of a year.

If she were going to be honest, all the good things happening for them were part of the reason she'd decided to take this step for herself. Maybe it was selfish to want a baby so desperately, but holding Lily felt so terribly *right*, as if a piece had settled into place inside her. She couldn't miss out on this chance just because she wasn't in a committed relationship—or *any* relationship at all.

Bri shared a glance with Ryan and shifted, twining a strand of her long, dark hair around a finger. "We really are happy for you. We're here anytime you need us."

"Yeah, like for Popsicles and Jell-O." Ryan grinned. "Bri couldn't get enough of those during her first trimester."

"I'm going to cross my fingers that I'm not laid up for months with morning sickness like she was." Avery laughed and finished off her beer. "But I'm not going to lie—I'm pretty damn relieved you all aren't passing out from shock and screaming about how this is all a big mistake. Drew excepted, of course."

He actually *growled*, though the tone was so low she didn't think anyone else heard. "Just because I'm the only one who sees reason doesn't mean I'm an ass."

"Yes, it does," all three of them chorused.

• • •

Drew ordered another round on the excuse of celebrating, but the truth was he just really needed a fucking drink. Avery was planning on getting knocked up? He couldn't wrap his mind around it. Yeah, she'd talked about having kids more and more over the last few years, but he'd always kind of thought she felt the same way he did about children—those things were much better in theory than in reality.

Apparently not.

He must have zoned out of the conversation, because the next thing he knew, Ryan sent him a sly look and asked, "So, Avery, who's the lucky guy you're going to knock boots with?"

Knock boots? What the fuck was wrong with his brother? Drew clenched his jaw and started looking for the waitress. Shots. He needed multiple shots of tequila or whiskey or something *right now*.

Bri's blue eyes went wide behind her cat-eye glasses. "Are you really going to do it that way? With someone we know?"

He couldn't begin to say why, but the thought of Avery having a baby with some douchebag from town made Drew want to shoot something. He knew better than anyone what kind of skeletons the people in Wellingford had in their closets. Most weren't crazy or dangerous, but that didn't mean he wanted Avery procreating with one of them. "You can't do that."

Avery frowned, a hint of challenge in her black eyes. "Says who?"

"Yeah, Drew—says who?" Ryan draped his arm over the back of the booth, and shot him a shit-eating grin. "Making a child is a very serious and profound experience."

The bastard. He was just trying to piss Drew off. "Exactly my point."

Bri snorted. "It's just what comes after that's less magical." As if on cue, Lily gurgled in a freakishly wet manner.

"Got it." His brother lifted the baby from her car seat, tossed a towel over his shoulder, and started patting her back. "She's been gassy for days. It's making all of us miserable."

"Not exactly the homecoming you wanted." Bri pulled out a giant diaper bag and rummaged through it.

"Honey, any homecoming involving you is exactly what I wanted."

His little brother looked at his new wife with such love

in his eyes that it damn near made Drew's teeth ache—even though this outcome was exactly what he'd wanted when he and Avery had set them up on a blind date.

He turned back to Avery. She was dressed the same as always, in her faded jeans and white T-shirt, with her straight black hair pulled back into a ponytail. He knew half a dozen guys off the top of his head who would give their left hand for a chance to date her. Having watched her grow from a gangly, awkward kid he used to tease into a stone cold stunner, he could see what got them all worked up. But they weren't talking about a date. They were talking about the rest of her life. "Avery, you can't do this."

"You keep saying that, and I keep hearing absolutely no legitimate reason why I can't. So say what you need to say, Flannery, or shut it."

"Well…" *Shit*. What the hell could he say? That the thought of her with another guy made him want to spit bullets? He caught the waitress's gaze and held up four fingers. Gena nodded, her blond hair bobbing around her face, and disappeared behind the bar. By the time Drew focused back on the table, Ryan was running his mouth again.

"Seriously, though, if you don't want to with someone at town, I'm still in contact with Jacks, even though he's a civilian now. I know for a fact last time he was here, all he could talk about was how impressed he was with your virtual driving skills."

Avery laughed again. "Now I know you're exaggerating. He whooped my ass in *Mario Kart*."

At the thought of Luke Jackson, the blond guy who'd come to visit Ryan last time he was home on leave, Drew almost growled again. The man had been all charm and smiles and had kept Avery tied up in conversation for the majority of the party at Chilly's. The fact that Jacks had had his knee blown out and replaced with an implant barely seemed to slow him down, though it had been severe enough for him to be honorably discharged from the pararescuers. Avery'd made an offhand comment about his impressive man-titties—really, who said man-titties—a few days later, which only cemented Drew's hatred. Had she seen his chest up close and personal? She hadn't mentioned that they'd seen each other again, let alone to play Wii. It made him wonder what else she left out…

Shit, he so wasn't going there.

"Those *are* some pretty fantastic genetics." Something came into her tone, something almost *dreamy*. "He'd make me a cute baby."

He couldn't do this. He couldn't sit here and listen to them talk about men like they were nothing but breeding stock. Especially not *that* one. Couldn't Avery see that the guy had a chip on his shoulder the size of Texas? He'd never be one to step up and help her with this baby shit. Hell, she'd be lucky if she heard from him again after the whole process. Process. What a clean way of talking about their knocking boots. "Jesus."

"Good God, Drew, I was just kidding." She glared at him. "You know I'm not going to go sleep with some testosterone-filled former pararescuer, no matter how attractive he is. Can you imagine the baby daddy drama that would come along with that?"

His brother's grin was aimed directly at Drew. "But think of the healthcare."

Drew glanced at Gena as she slid four more beers onto

the table. "Whiskey. Straight up."

"Sure thing."

He turned back to find them all staring at him. "What?" Even as he asked, he knew exactly what their problem was. Given the golden Flannery history, both he and Ryan stayed away from the hard stuff. *Screw it*. He couldn't get through this conversation without doing *something* to save his sanity.

Ryan grabbed his beer and lifted it in Avery's direction. "Well, I'm really happy for you. You might be crazy, but you're going to be a good mom."

Of course Bri and Ryan were being supportive. They had a baby and stars in their eyes. They weren't thinking about the fact that Avery would be doing this as a single mother. That shit changed everything, made even the smallest trials a hundred times harder.

Avery laughed. "Wow, Ryan. Thanks for that."

His brother was right, though. Drew's new niece might freak him out because she was so tiny and angry and breakable, but Avery never seemed to have a problem doing the various tasks associated with a kid. And she already had a decent setup for a kid—a business she owned that was only open regular store hours, a cozy little house in a decent neighborhood, a close-knit system of friends. She was financially stable, but if his brother's kid had taught him anything, it was that babies were expensive. They needed so much *stuff*. Some random asshole sperm donor wasn't going to help out there, and he doubted she would even consider asking.

And what happened if the kid got sick? Medical bills were a bitch in a big way. Was the baby daddy going to sweep in and help out? Drew didn't think so. *He'd* be the one there for her, financially and otherwise, while she raised some other dude's spawn.

He might as well be the one who got the perks to go with the burden. And those were some huge fucking perks. He watched her out of the corner of his eye. Avery might be forbidden territory, but that hadn't ever stopped him from *thinking* about her like that.

Drew took another pull from his beer and discarded the idea. That was too crazy, even for him. He couldn't volunteer to be Avery's sperm donor.

Could he?

The conversation around the table pulled his attention outward again. "And just think—I'll be able to read to your baby and Lily, and they can spend time in the library with me, and grow up being best friends. It'll be so amazing watching those two discover the books they love." Bri was practically clapping her hands with glee. "Oh, this will be *perfect*."

"You do realize that this will be years in the making, right? It takes nine months for the baby to even get here." Avery jerked a thumb in her friend's direction and gave Ryan a meaningful look. "Sounds like she's jonesing for another baby, hoss. You better get on that."

His brother got a little wide around the eyes, his calm breaking for the first time since Avery had come out with her news. "Lily isn't even sleeping through the night. How about we take things one step at a time?"

The three of them laughed, but Drew couldn't make himself join in. Those two thought this was great, and Avery only had the endgame in mind. None of them were considering what her life would be like once that baby finally showed up. *He* was the only one looking that far ahead.

And he didn't like what he saw.

The truth settled in his chest, making him feel both lighter and heavier at the same time. If he didn't step in, some asshole would leave her high and dry. She needed someone who was going to be there for her. Someone she could call if she got in over her head financially, or if she needed to blow off some steam, or even if she needed a good cry. He couldn't remember the last time he'd seen actual tears in her eyes.

No, that wasn't true. He knew the exact day and time Avery had last shed a tear. It was when she found out that she had the same genetic flags as both her mother and sister. He stared at his beer. Avery had been stronger than strong since then, but Bri had burst into tears at the most inane shit when she was pregnant.

A random guy wasn't going to be able to be there for her.

Drew could. Hell, he'd make sure the actual getting-pregnant process was good for her, too. A stranger couldn't guarantee that.

Avery had been his rock in a childhood where he was forced to grow up before his time. No matter what shit his dad put him through, or how hard things got, she helped him lose himself in made-up competitions and mad schemes. She was a constant in all his childhood memories, from the day she'd shoved him down in grade school after he made her sister cry by asking why her Chinese eyes were strange. And then, horrified when *he* started to cry too, Avery had offered her hand and told him they were going to be best friends.

If he did this, it wouldn't be about starting a family and creating a life with someone. It would be about being there for his best friend like she'd always been there for him.

"Earth to Drew." Ryan waved a hand in front of his face. His little brother frowned down at the shot glass on the table between them. "Your drink is here."

He didn't need it anymore, not with the plan coming together in his head. "I've got to go."

"Just like that?" Avery frowned. "I know you're pissed, but you don't have to storm off."

"I'm not storming." He reached over and patted her shoulder, the innocent touch not feeling quite so innocent with the turn his thoughts had taken. "I forgot I had to do something. I'll talk to you later." *When Bri and Ryan weren't there to witness and offer commentary.*

"Sure. See you later."

He could feel all their eyes on him as he cut through the tables scattered across Chilly's floor and headed for the door. He needed to soften Avery up before he made his pitch. She wasn't going to be easy to convince, but he planned to pull out all the stops to make her see that this was the only logical solution.

Drew would be the sperm donor. It was as simple as that.

Chapter Two

After Avery waved goodbye to Ryan and Bri, it hit her that for all her bravado, she had no idea what she was doing. Hell, she hadn't even told her family yet. *Yé-ye* was going to lose his shit over the choice to do in vitro fertilization, let alone if she picked a donor who wasn't one hundred percent Chinese. Maybe she'd finally surpass Alexis as the so-called "failure" of the family.

God, what if she wasn't ready for this?

Avery shook her head and climbed up into her Jeep. It didn't matter. The time to waffle about this was long past. She'd made her decision, and she was going to stick with it. Being a mother *was* a big step, but it felt too right for her to let that dream go. And, strangely enough, moving forward with getting pregnant made her feel closer to her mother.

Even now, fifteen years later, she still missed Mom. The tightness in her chest had never really left after that winter when her mother fought cancer and lost. She'd been in remission for nearly five years, and then a routine test came back positive. Six months later, she was gone, wasted away before their eyes.

Avery wiped a stray tear from her eyes. She'd gotten to say her goodbyes, had been able to hold her hand while Mom told her how proud she was, and how sure she was that Avery would grow up to be as wonderful a woman as she was a child. It was world's better than what Bri had gone through—waving goodbye to parents who would never come home again because of a horrific car accident. Or Drew, for that matter, losing his mom when he was only five. That was bad enough, but Drew's father had slowly checked out on their family, turning more and more to the booze that morphed him from a gruff man to the mean son of a gun who made his boys' lives a living hell.

On days like today, she wondered what her mother would think of her. Would she be proud Avery wasn't taking her fate lying down? Or would she be disappointed because she wasn't willing to wait for the man of her dreams to come along, and then adopt? She'd never know.

God, could she get any mopier?

She pulled onto her street and cursed. What was Drew doing here? As much as she cared about the guy, she didn't really feel up to his bitching about her life choices right now. She put some serious thought into driving past her house and going…pretty much anywhere else…but this conversation had to happen sooner or later. Might as well get it over with.

The smell of coffee hit her as she walked through the front door, and she nearly moaned when she realized that he'd brought out the good stuff. Which meant he was apologizing…or about to step up his argument to the next level.

There was something else, though. Something that smelled suspiciously like onions. She stopped short in the archway into her kitchen. "What are you doing?"

Drew glanced up, a giant knife in his hand. "I'm chopping vegetables."

Yeah, which was what had her scared. "Dude, you can't cook."

"No shit, really?" He rolled his eyes. "I wasn't going to touch your blessed stove. I just figured I'd get things started so you had less to do when you got home. Coffee?"

Avery was afraid to step into the kitchen and be sucked into whatever alternate dimension that had spit out this domestic version of Drew. She took a step sideways, searching the room for evidence of something terrible having happened—like a personality-changing blow to the head. "Who did you kill?"

"What?"

"Seriously, whose body do you need help burying in the woods?"

The confusion in his blue eyes cleared. "If I had to bury a body, I wouldn't call your ass. Your damn Jeep would probably break down in the middle of nowhere and we'd get stranded—and caught."

"Bite your tongue. The Beast would never do such a thing." She stepped into the kitchen and accepted the cup he offered. If he was verbally sparring with her, then things couldn't be that shitty. "So, what's the deal? You usually show up and demand to be fed, and then hang out drinking my beer while I do all the work."

"Only because after the last time, you threatened to cut off my hand if I touched anything in here again."

"You lit my house on fire! I thought Ryan was supposed to be the pyro in the family."

Drew shrugged. "It was only a tiny grease fire."

"You burnt up my curtains."

"You never liked those curtains to begin with. And I *did* buy you new ones." He put on his most charming smile, the one that she called the panty-dropper after seeing it charm women into going home with him from Chilly's more times than she really wanted to think about. It was a good look for him, with his longish, curly dark hair, five o'clock shadow, and piercing blue eyes. She'd never told him it affected her on nearly the same level, too. There'd be no living with him if he knew.

Besides, being with Drew like *that* wasn't in the cards for her.

She drank her coffee, trying to keep the pleasure she got from the taste off her face. He was up to something and she wasn't about to roll over and play dead for him. "Back to my original question—what's going on?"

"Does something have to be going on for your best friend to come over and start dinner for you?"

"One, if it's you, yes. Two, twenty-odd minutes ago you stormed off without so much as an explanation, so *hell yes*. Stop playing dumb and spit it out." Because if she drank too much of this coffee, she was going to be in danger of agreeing to damn near anything he put forward.

"For the last time, I didn't storm off. I needed to think." Drew took a deep breath, suddenly serious in a way that made her heart beat faster. "I want to be the one you do this with."

Avery stared, wondering if a jet engine had just taken off in her kitchen. It was the only way to explain the roaring in her ears. No way had he just said what she thought he just said. His lips might have moved, but that had to be some messed up hallucination taking over and putting words that he'd never actually say into his mouth. "Um…what?"

"You know…" He waved his hand as if that really meant something. "Your sperm donor or baby daddy or whatever the hell you want to call it."

The coffee she'd just drunk did something unpleasant in her stomach. "Are you screwing with me right now? Because I knew your sense of humor was out of whack, but this is beyond not okay."

"Jesus, Avery, will you just listen to me? I'm serious as a heart attack." He looked it, but that didn't mean a damn thing. Not when they were talking about Drew, King of Practical Jokes and Wellingford's most eligible bachelor.

She shook her head. "You were just yelling at me about how this is the worst mistake of my life. While it'd be great if you suddenly had an epiphany where you changed your mind, that doesn't happen in real life—not in twenty minutes."

"It's not like that." He scrubbed his hand over his face. "Look, I was just reacting before. You kind of sprang the whole 'I'm having a baby' thing on me out of nowhere, and then hearing you'd actually consider doing it with some stranger… I lost my shit, okay? I'm sorry."

There had never been any possibility of her doing it with a stranger, and the fact he'd been so ready to believe she would pissed her off something fierce. "It's great to know you have such a high opinion of me."

"That's not fair."

"What's not fair is you assuming I'm just going to sleep around until some lucky sperm finds my egg. Maybe throw in a gangbang to make sure it really sticks." God, she was so angry, she actually considered throwing her coffee at him. "You're such a dick."

He swore. "I'm not saying this right."

"You think?" Maybe she'd eventually be able to laugh about his thinking the worst of her and offering something so insane. *Maybe*. In like ten years.

Drew took a deep breath, and she recognized it for the jumping off point it was. "Just hear me out, okay?"

The more he talked, the closer she got to sacrificing the insanely good coffee and tossing it in his face. "You have thirty seconds before I kick your ass. Make them count."

He set the knife on the counter and slid it behind him—out of her reach. Smart man. "If you use some random donor, then you're on your own. It's all on you. Yeah, you have a great support system between your family and friends, but the burden still falls squarely on you."

"You think I don't know that?" She'd lost sleep agonizing over this choice, and he seemed to think she'd just woke up one day and decided to bang her way through the entire town to get knocked up. "I'm done listening—"

He held up his hand. "I have fifteen seconds left. I'm not exactly Father of the Year material, but I have a steady job and I can be there when the strain gets to be too much. Even if you don't want the kid to know who their dad is, I'll still at least help you financially. Please, Avery. Let me help you."

That stopped her cold. She took a sip of coffee and

forced down her emotional knee-jerk reaction. He wasn't being a dick. Okay, he kind of was. But this was coming from a good place, even if his delivery was off. "Drew, you don't have to take care of me anymore. I'm twenty-seven years old and I own my own business. I'm doing just fine."

"I know that. Christ, I know that. You don't need a babysitter." He looked around her kitchen as if the answer to some question was hidden in her cabinets. "Sweetheart, I've been there with you through all of it. *I* was the one who camped out with you in that old tree house for days on end and held you after your mom died. It was *me* who sat with you while we waited for your sister to come out of the surgery that cut out her cancer. *I* was the one holding your hand while we waited for those test results to come back, and I was the one who supplied the alcohol to get you drunk, and the shoulder to cry on while you processed it. I understand. You don't have to do this alone."

God. He really knew where to hit her to make her feel like an ass. It didn't make any sense. *He* was the one being irrational, from his protesting that this was a terrible idea to his offer to be a sperm donor. For all his accusations, he was the one who hadn't thought things through.

But that was Drew. He knew when she was hurting or in trouble, and he didn't hesitate to ride to the rescue. It shouldn't have surprised her that he'd do the same thing in this situation. "This isn't some game of pretend. This is the real thing. There might be questions later on about who the daddy is. You prepared to deal with that?"

He met her gaze, and there was no hesitation in his blue eyes. "Like I said, I'm not going to be Father of the Year, but if the kid has questions, I'm going to be there to answer them—however you want to handle it. It'll be your choice."

Shit. She could actually feel her resolve crumbling against the weight of his sincerity. "Drew… This is a big decision to make. Maybe you need to take a day—or a month—to really think about it." *She* needed time to think about it. It was one thing to use a sperm donor who was only a list of characteristics and a number label. Using someone she *knew* was a totally different story.

But…he had a point. And it wasn't like the experience would be different for her, no matter who donated the sperm. Two appointments, a simple procedure, thirty minutes on her back, and she was good to go. Drew wouldn't even have to be in the room—he could save his support for before and after.

She bit her lip. Recent issues aside, he was the standard she held all other men against. She couldn't have picked a better man if she'd tried.

So why not Drew himself?

"I don't need the time to think," he said. "The offer is on the table and it's going to stay there. It's up to you to decide what you want."

Chapter Three

Drew held his breath while she sipped her coffee. It wasn't that he thought Avery would accept his offer without any questions—he just hadn't thought *he'd* be so stressed about her answer.

And she seemed to actually be *thinking* about it, which he hadn't expected.

He fought the urge to fidget. He'd never met anyone with a stare quite as unnerving as Avery's. He'd once told her that she should join the department, and he'd only been half joking. If he put her in a room with even the hardest redneck asshole, the guy would break inside of fifteen minutes. Hell, *he* was starting to sweat and he hadn't done a damn thing wrong.

Except act like an ass and then turn around and make an offer that was nearly as crazy as her plan to begin with. But that was their gig—they came up with insane plots. Look what they'd done with Ryan and Bri. Normal people wouldn't be willing to strand their friends in a cabin for three days to force them to admit how perfect they were for each other.

But Drew and Avery had never been normal people.

He had a moment of wondering why the hell he was so determined to make this happen, and then she was nodding. "Okay. Let's do it."

"Okay?" He could hardly dare hope she was actually agreeing to it. She was willing to go to bed with him and make an actual baby? The thought of *his* child growing inside her stomach made the room waver around him. He wanted to pull her into his arms and haul her ass to the bedroom to get this started, but he killed the urge. This wasn't about him seducing her—this was just him being a good friend. Maybe not all friends would make the same offer he just had, but most people weren't as close as he and Avery were.

Her dark hair slid over her shoulder as she bent to examine the veggies he'd chopped, which led his mind right into the gutter, imagining how it'd look spread out over his pillow. From there it was a slippery slope right into checking out the way her small breasts filled out that white T-shirt, and how her jeans clung damn near lovingly to her ass. She looked *good* in her clothes. It was only logical that she'd look even better out of them.

Wait. She said yes.

He was going to have sex with Avery Yeung.

Sweat broke out on his forehead. Would she arch against him when he touched her? He'd heard the sounds she made when she drank that coffee she loved so much. Would she make the same ones while he tasted her? Drew's mouth watered at the thought of having her spread out and there for the taking.

Fuck. This is really happening. He opened the fridge and pulled out two beers with shaking hands. After opening both, he handed her one and raised his in a toast. "To making babies?"

"Let's not get ahead of ourselves." Avery laughed, though she looked a little pale. "To making *a* baby."

• • •

Avery had obviously lost what little sense God gave her, if she was agreeing to this. Either that, or some latent *something* for Drew was doubling her daily dose of stupidity. Whatever the reason, she couldn't bring herself to change her mind as she clinked her bottle against his.

They looked at each other as they drank, their silence threatening to become awkward. The way he was looking at her, dark eyes so intense and filled with things she couldn't put a name to…it was even hotter than his panty-dropper smile. She hadn't thought there *could* be anything hotter than his panty-dropper smile, but she'd underestimated those eyes of his. What if he offered to create a baby the old fashioned way? She could imagine all too well what it'd feel like if he pressed against her in a way that had nothing to do with friendship.

Whoa. She shook her head. That was the fast train to overthinking things.

"Now, about dinner…" He ran his fingers through his hair, and she didn't miss the fact his hand was shaking a little, or that sweat dotted his temples. It shouldn't comfort her that he was just as nervous at taking this step as she was, but it did. It was good to know he hadn't made this decision lightly.

Time to take control of the situation.

"God, you're a mess." She pushed him away from the cutting board and stove. "You can barely chop vegetables. What would your brother say?"

"Same thing he always does—get out of my kitchen."

"Man after my own heart." Though her father had taught her to cook, Ryan had been forced to learn so he and Drew wouldn't starve—or eat the only thing Drew could manage that was edible: grilled cheese sandwiches.

She shook off the unhappy thought, and her mind drifted back to the fantasy she always avoided like the plague. Drew. With her. Would he make her feel soft and feminine? Or would he toss her around like a Viking with his conquest? She didn't know which she'd prefer, only that thinking about it brought her blood to a simmer. He was so much taller than her five feet, two inches that he'd dwarf her in the bedroom.

It would make sixty-nine a lot easier, though.

"What are you thinking about so hard over there?"

She dropped the bowl she'd been sliding the vegetables into, sending them scattering over the linoleum floor. "Shit."

As she sank to her knees, she hoped to God the bad lighting was enough to hide the furious blush she could feel staining her cheeks and neck.

"Are you okay?" He went to his knees next to her, helping gather up the onion and pepper and cauliflower pieces and put them back into the bowl.

"Fine. Just clumsy." And an idiot for entertaining thoughts of a naked Drew, even for a second. She'd seen the writing on the wall when he'd made little Kelsey Volsom cry because he'd kissed her and then told her he wouldn't be her boyfriend.

Though there *had* been one night in high school where things could have gone *there*, Avery had managed to remember all the reasons they couldn't before Drew kissed her. She needed Drew too desperately to run the risk of losing him forever because of some stupid sex stuff.

Even if, over the years, she sometimes found herself lying in the dark and touching herself while picturing someone who bore a striking resemblance to her best friend.

He put his hand over hers, shorting out her thoughts. "Avery, breathe. They're just vegetables. I know you're stressed about everything you're going through, but you need to take a deep breath."

How the hell was she supposed to take a deep breath when all she could smell was *him*? And, God, he smelled amazing, fresh and clean like the air in Wellingford, their little Pennsylvania town.

Stop it. Stop it right now. He isn't interested in you like that, and he's never going to be. Being your baby's daddy only means he's a good friend, not that he's harboring the same twisted fantasies about you that you do about him. He's going to jizz in a cup, for God's sake.

By the time she looked up to meet his gaze, she had control of her emotions. This wasn't the Drew who'd made her think filthy thoughts when her guard was down. This was her best friend. The best friend who was going to donate sperm for a totally clinical procedure. *Nope, nothing sexy about that. Thank God.*

Avery smiled. "I'm fine. Seriously. Just a little frazzled."

"How about we call the whole dinner thing off and just

order pizza?"

She could do this. "Only if you throw some *Mario Kart* into it."

"Loser pays?"

"Don't they always?" Yes, *this* was the norm. Not the weird sexual tension that had just shown up, and not thoughts of being naked and sweaty with Drew. Just this. Them, being there for each other through thick and thin. They could deal with everything else later.

"Deal." He dumped the veggies into the trash and held out a hand to haul her to her feet. "Now move your ass, Yeung. I'm starving."

Chapter Four

Drew paced his living room Monday morning, pausing to check his reflection in the mirror. He'd pulled out all the stops for this, had even found a pair of slacks in the back of his closet and a button-up shirt that didn't have too many wrinkles. The man staring back at him didn't look like Drew. *He* didn't dress up or go through this level of effort for anyone, let alone a woman.

But Avery wasn't just any woman. She was *Avery*. And if he was going to do this, he was going to do this right.

It would just be a hell of a lot easier if his stomach would settle the fuck down.

He crossed to the beat-up coffee table where he'd left his phone, knocking over the stack of *Sports Illustrated* as he rechecked the text message for the twentieth time.

Meet me at two at my place.

It was happening. He was finally going to sleep with Avery Yeung. It'd been something he spent a lot of long summer nights thinking about when she turned fifteen and puberty hit, which felt a lot like he woke up one day and his best friend was a *girl*. A hot one.

But the one time he'd made a move after they shared a case of beer they'd stolen from his father, she'd told him in no uncertain terms that it was never going to happen. And, once he sobered up, he'd more than agreed with her. His longest relationship hadn't come close to six months before it ended. They *all* ended at some point. He couldn't risk losing Avery. So he never brought it up again.

Which wasn't to say he never *thought* about it again.

Before he could second-guess himself and his decision, he grabbed his keys and headed out the door. The ten-minute drive to her place seemed to take both too long and not nearly long enough. He found her sitting on her front porch, doing something that looked suspiciously like wringing her hands.

She was also wearing a pair of yoga pants and a tank top.

What the fuck? He was standing there like an idiot, wearing slacks. He might as well have printed out a sign that said, "Trying too hard" and stapled it to his forehead. He was making too big a deal of this, and his clothes broadcasted that fact.

She glanced up when he got out of his car. "We're going to be late."

"Late?" He hadn't been aware he was on a timetable. Some things weren't meant to be rushed. Drew wiped his palms on his slacks, trying not to fidget when she pinned him with a look.

"Yeah, late. Come on. I'll drive." She practically herded him into the passenger seat of the Beast and then climbed into the driver's side.

What the hell was going on?

He didn't get his explanation until ten minutes later when she pulled into the parking lot of a fertility clinic. Drew stared at the tasteful sign above the door. Why the fuck were they here? "My swimmers are fine."

"What?" She shut off her Jeep.

"My swimmers." He gestured at his lap, wanting to growl when her eyes went wide. "They're fine. More than able to get the job done."

"Uh… I have no doubt of that." She looked like she wanted to be doing anything else but having this conversation. "This is just one of the necessary steps. It's not because I think your, ah, swimmers aren't up to snuff."

Necessary steps. So she must want him to get some tests done or some shit. Drew took a deep breath. He'd said he was down for this, and that meant doing whatever so-called necessary steps Avery needed. Even though it was *not* necessary as far as he was concerned. He was thirty, not even past his prime.

Whatever. He'd go through whatever tests she needed. Then they'd go back to her place and get this baby-making business started.

He hopped out of the Jeep, but she was already out of the driver's seat before he had a chance to open her door for her. Which he probably wouldn't have done if it wasn't for what they were going to do in the near future.

Fuck, I'm still overthinking this.

He followed her through the clinic door and up to the counter, since she obviously knew where she was going.

She handed him a clipboard with paperwork. "You need

to fill this out."

Okay. Fill out paperwork. He supposed it would make sense that she'd want to know his medical and family history—though she should have known all of it already. He dropped into one of the plain plastic chairs and diligently went about answering a whole lot of uncomfortable questions. By the time he reached the last one, he was ready to haul ass out of there.

Avery apparently had different plans. She re-crossed her legs, one foot bouncing as she pointed at the seat next to her, which he'd just vacated.

With a sigh, he sat down again, his attention straying to the women—and a few men—who occupied the waiting room. Nearly to a person, they looked ill at ease and stressed. The women with men held their partners' hands, though he couldn't tell if it was for comfort or because they simply wanted to.

"Drew Flannery."

He jumped, and then stood up when Avery did and followed her to the plump, older nurse. She smiled at them, making him wonder if she were someone's grandmother—the kind who made cookies and read bedtime stories and…

What the hell was he even thinking?

As soon as they turned the corner from the waiting room, she handed him a small clear cup that had a sticker with his information on it. "You'll put the specimen in here, please."

The nurse opened a door. "You can leave the cup in the room when you're done." She smiled at Avery. "You're welcome to go into the room with him, but we ask that you ensure there's no saliva or other fluids involved so you don't contaminate the specimen."

Avery made a choked noise. "That's *so* not going to be a problem."

The nurse laughed and patted her shoulder. "I've heard that one before, honey. I'll just leave you to it."

He barely waited for her to disappear back around the corner before he turned to examine the room. It looked like an entire frat house's stash of porn had exploded in there. "Isn't this a little much for a few tests?"

She looked at him like he was an idiot. "How else are you going to get your engine running? Besides, this isn't about tests—though I'm sure they'll run a few. You wanted to help me make a baby, so let's make a baby. Now go get 'em, champ."

Jesus Christ. She expected him to leave a *specimen* so the doctor could shoot it up her... Apparently when they'd talked about making a baby, something had gotten lost in translation. "You're shitting me."

"Nope." She slid past him into the room and meandered around, stopping in front of the television and eyeing the collection of DVDs on the shelf next to it. "Oh, look, they have *Busty Blondes #37*. I seem to remember you having one of these videos back in high school."

He grabbed her shoulders and tried to steer her away from the shelf. "Not interested." Truth was, his inspiration for self-sessions had migrated toward pretty Asian women who looked a whole lot like the one standing in the room with him.

"If you're not into the DVDs, they have magazines, too." She poked one with her finger. "Though this one appears a bit crusty."

"Christ, stop touching things. Do you know what men do in here?"

She rolled her eyes. "Yeah, Drew, that's kind of the point. They come in here, watch or read whatever tickles their fancy, and then masturbate into that sanitary little cup right there."

When she said 'masturbate' he thought his head might actually explode. "Avery—"

"Are you worried about hitting your mark? That cup *is* kind of a small. Want me to go find something bigger?"

God, she was killing him. It would have been so much more bearable if he thought she was kidding, but Avery was drop dead serious. It was a sign of her nervousness that she hadn't cracked a joke since he got into her Jeep.

He couldn't do it.

Not like this. "This is wrong."

"This clinic has a ninety percent success rate—better than most in the state. There's nothing *wrong* about those odds." She motioned at the cup again. "So get to it."

Get to it. Just like that. He grabbed her hand. "We're leaving."

"Leaving? But—"

"*Now.*"

• • •

Avery wasn't sure where it all went sideways. Drew seemed fine—if a bit quiet—while they were waiting, but then he'd lost his shit as soon as they got into the room. She stopped in the parking lot. "Drew—"

"Give me your keys." He snatched them out of her hand.

"Get in the damn Jeep."

He'd gone off the deep end. "Why are you—?"

Drew looked at her, and she went still at the anger on his face. "Shut up and get in the car."

She hurried around the hood, worried that he'd actually leave her behind if she didn't pick up the pace. He nearly took out a car when he shot out of the parking lot, but she bit her lip instead of commenting on a member of the Sheriff's department breaking all sorts of speed limits as they flew down the country roads back toward Wellingford.

God help her, but she'd become pretty damn attached to the idea of Drew being the one who made the other half of this baby. Maybe his backing out was for the best, but she couldn't stem a rush of disappointment knowing this wouldn't be happening.

What was she supposed to say? There wasn't exactly an entry for this kind of situation in Miss Manners. She took a deep breath as he jerked into her driveway and slammed on the brakes. "Well, thanks for trying anyway. I get why you… why you're not okay with it."

He stared down at his clenched hands. Or maybe he was counting the scars on his fingers. She had no way of knowing. Finally, Drew spoke, his voice so low she could barely hear him. "I'm not going to come in a cup and then have some doctor implant you with a turkey baster."

"Uh…that's not exactly how it works." Wow, this was getting more awkward by the second. "I get it. You freaked out. It's really okay. It's not even going to affect the appointment I have set up next week. They'll just use the donor I'd already picked out."

"No." Just that. No explanation, no reasoning, nothing

but that freakishly calm expression. She opened her mouth to keep arguing, but Drew got out of the Beast and slammed the door. Though she half expected him to storm over to his truck and head for home, he marched around to her side of the Jeep and yanked open her door. "Come on."

"What?"

He grabbed her arm and hauled her down, not holding her tightly enough to hurt, but she wasn't getting away without a fight. Avery stumbled along next to him, confusion deepening with each step. What had crawled up his ass this time? She hadn't locked the door, so there was no pause on her porch before he towed her inside, finally stopping in her kitchen.

She jerked her arm out of his grasp. "What's wrong with you?" When he didn't immediately answer, she had to fight the urge to deck him. "You can't just—" She broke off as he stepped into her space, so close their chests almost brushed.

Drew met her gaze, his blue eyes full of something she wasn't sure she wanted to define. "Avery, shut up and listen to me. If we're going to do this—and we are—we're going to do this *right*."

And then he kissed her.

Chapter Five

Drew Flannery was kissing her. No. Kissing wasn't a strong enough word for what he was doing. He *claimed* her lips, tongue thrusting into her mouth as if it had every right to be there.

God help her, but Avery wasn't sure it didn't.

She melted against him, her hands going to his chest and touching him in a way she'd never dreamed would be reality. He was so hard and warm and, oh lord, his hands gripped her hips, jerking her tighter against him and eliminating what tiny space there'd been to begin with. But he wasn't done. Drew pulled her shirt off in a swift move that barely broke their kiss.

He nipped her bottom lip, sending zings through her entire body. His hands were everywhere—her back to unhook her bra, down her spine, grabbing her ass and grinding her against him.

"*Avery*," he groaned against her mouth. "Holy *shit*."

Holy shit is right.

She dug her fingers into his hair and gave herself over to kissing him back, looping one leg around his waist so he could rub that hard length exactly where she needed him.

The sheer sensory overload pushed her damn near to the edge. She rocked, but the friction only heightened her need. They had to get out of these clothes. Immediately.

Apparently he was thinking the same thing, because he kissed his way down her jaw to her neck and lower. The sight of *Drew's* mouth trailing kisses between her breasts was too much, so she closed her eyes and focused on just feeling. And, God, it felt good. Better than good.

He worked off her yoga pants and laughed. "Wonder Woman?"

She opened her eyes again, this time to glare. "This wasn't even in my realm of possibilities today — or *ever* — so, yeah, I have my really awesome Wonder Woman briefs on."

"I like them." He sat back on his heels and just looked at her, his gaze tracing over her face, to her breasts and down to her feet. Despite wearing only underwear, she hadn't felt naked until that moment.

What the ever loving fuck were they doing? She should put an end to this situation immediately. Even if it was miles better than her fantasies.

Avery started to cross her arms over her chest, but he leaned forward and nipped her hipbone, sending more of those delicious sparks through her. She nearly jumped out of her skin when he did it on the other side, a whimper slipping free. "*Drew.*"

"I've got you, sweetheart." His voice was hoarse, his lips barely leaving her skin.

Her panties slid down her legs, helped along by his teeth. Oh God, was he really going there? She bit her lip against the need to beg him not to stop. "You really don't have to—"

He looked up and met her gaze, his blue eyes gone dark with something like need. "I want to."

• • •

Drew ran his tongue along the curve of her thigh. She tasted like the best kind of drug, and her sharply indrawn breath only spurred him on. He wanted to make her feel good, but more than that, he wanted to finally satisfy the insane fascination he'd held for Avery ever since he could remember.

What kind of sounds would she make as she came?

Only one way to find out.

He pushed her against the counter, needing to taste her even though he damn well knew he should get her ass in bed. But he couldn't wait that long. "Christ, Avery, you have no idea how much I want this." He dragged his tongue over her wetness. It was so much better than anything conjured by his imagination. Another lick only confirmed it. He needed this, needed her. With a groan, he gave himself over to everything that was Avery, exploring her with his mouth, reveling in her taste, her cries, the feeling of her fingers twisting in his hair. Her hips bucked as she tried to move against his mouth, but he pinned her in place as he circled his tongue over her clit.

"There. Like that. Oh my God, *don't stop*."

There wasn't a chance in hell of that. "I'm not stopping until you come. And maybe not even then."

He fought to keep his pace consistent and hold her still as her cries grew more and more frantic. So close. She was about to come, and *he* was the cause. Driven by desperation akin to what she had to be feeling, he let go of her hip with one hand and pushed a finger into her. He growled at how tight she was, loving how she clenched around him. She dug her fingers into his hair, a scream slipping free, and rode out the orgasm.

His body shaking more than it had a right to, he climbed to his feet. Now was the time to get to a goddamn bedroom. But then she looked up at him, her dark eyes cloudy with desire, and his plan wavered. "Sweetheart, you're not making this easy on me."

"This is your fault." She licked her lips, and it was all the invitation he needed. Drew kissed her, his need overtaking anything else. A bed? He'd be lucky if he got out of his pants before he was inside her.

He hooked the back of her legs and lifted her onto the kitchen counter, pausing only to palm her breasts, each topped with a dusky nipple just begging for his mouth. Christ. She was just as perfect here as she was everywhere else.

"Hurry up," she breathed.

"I'm hurrying, woman. Jesus." Drew tried to pull off his shirt, but fumbling with the buttons made him feel more like snarling. Luckily, his pants weren't as much trouble, and he shoved them down and stepped up to pull her to the edge of the counter. He could actually *see* how wet she was, and her breasts bounced a little with each jagged breath.

But before he could get to the good stuff, she put a hand on his chest. "Um, maybe we should talk diseases right now."

Fuck. With his history, it made sense for her to ask, but he hated that she had to, even if it was his own damn fault.

He ran his hands up the tops of her thighs and back down again. "I'm clean. I'm always careful and I get tested on the regular, just to be safe." Not to mention he didn't get around nearly as much as everyone seemed to think. Not anymore.

"Okay."

All he wanted to do was shove home and stay there until neither one of them could move, but he found himself saying, "Last chance. You sure about this?" If she had any doubts, now was the time to call the whole thing off.

"Oh no. You don't get to take the goddamn noble route now." She hooked the back of his neck and brought his head down until their noses damn near touched. Avery glared, though the effect was kind of ruined by the aftereffects of her orgasm, apparent on her face. "Finish this, or I'm going to kick your ass."

"Thank Christ." He spread her legs wide and shoved into her, sheathing himself to the hilt. They both froze, her eyes as glazed as his felt. This was it. He was inside Avery Yeung—*bareback* inside her—and, God help him, but it was fucking perfect. Though he couldn't be sure, Drew thought he heard a chorus of baby angels singing, though that very well could have been him losing his damn mind over how good it felt. It struck him that this was the first time he'd ever had sex without a condom, and how right it was that it should be with her. But then the thought was swept away by the sensation of her clenching around his cock.

"Oh my God," she moaned. She tried to move, but he easily kept her still with his hands on her hips. She made a frustrated noise. "You are such a fucking tease."

"I'm trying not to *hurt* you." His voice came out nearly as breathy as hers. "Stop talking so much." He kissed her as he moved, withdrawing almost completely before he thrust deep again. When she wrapped her legs around his waist, his already damaged control snapped.

He drew back and shoved in, again and again, and her position left her helpless to do anything but take it. Not that she seemed to mind. She kissed him back with a ferocity he could only have dreamed of, her tongue sliding along his before she set her teeth into his lip, making him moan. Her nails dug into his back, urging him on, much the same way as her heels against his ass.

As if there were any chance of him backing off now.

No, he was lost for sure.

Drew changed his angle so he rubbed against her clit on every other stroke, gritting his teeth to keep a consistent rhythm as she went wild around him.

"God, oh God, Drew, please. *Ahh*."

The strength of her orgasm pulled him into his own, and he thrust harder, grinding against her as he emptied himself. For one insane moment, he wondered if she was taking more than just his physical release, but the thought passed before he could analyze it. Breathing hard, he let his forehead rest against hers.

Holy shit. Whatever he'd expected when he'd agreed to this thing, it wasn't *this*. He'd just had sex with Avery. His best friend, his partner in crime, the one person in this world who knew all his secrets.

And, worst of all, he wanted to do it again.

Chapter Six

Avery sat on her kitchen counter and tried to remember how to breathe. God, that was amazing. She couldn't remember the last time she'd been with someone who made her feel so... Words escaped her. Something intense. Really intense.

She rested her head on his shoulder and inhaled deeply. The familiar cologne had her eyes flying back open. Holy shit, what had she done? Sex. In her kitchen. With Drew. She closed her eyes and then opened them again, but he didn't vanish like he should have, if this was all a vivid hallucination. Yep, that definitely happened.

"Shit." She snatched her hands from his chest—his seriously sexy chest—but that didn't do a damn thing about the fact they were still connected in the most intimate way possible. *And, holy hell, the rumor mill wasn't exaggerating about his...assets.* He still hadn't met her gaze, but that was probably for the best. What was she supposed to say? *Thanks for the bang. Uh...please leave now because I can't wrap my mind around the fact that you, Drew Flannery, are inside me right now.*

Actually, that sounded pretty perfect.

She used two fingers against his sternum to push him back a step, and the feel of him sliding from her body almost drew another whimper of protest from her. Good sex had a way of doing that to a person, right? It certainly wasn't that she wanted more of what they'd just been doing. Nope.

There wasn't nearly enough space between them, but she couldn't stand sitting there with her legs spread to kingdom come a second longer. She slid off the counter and moved sideways, needing to put some distance between them. "Well, thanks."

He blinked as if just waking up. Hell, maybe he was. It was the only explanation for what had just happened. Either that or her sex-starved brain had taken her midnight fantasies to a whole new level.

Drew shook his head. "Sure thing. My pleasure."

Yeah, totally sounded like it. This was too weird. Apparently he thought so, too, because he rubbed a hand over his face and shook himself again. "So…I'll see you tomorrow?"

"Sure." She bit her lip, silently begging him to leave so they could stop this awkward conversation that threatened to stretch out forever if someone didn't do something. "I'll call you."

"Works for me." He scooped his pants off the floor and pulled them on, looking a little unsteady on his feet. That was great—she wasn't feeling too steady herself. He slipped into his shirt, but it was wrinkled beyond saving. He didn't bother to button it.

That little slice of chest visible nearly had her saying to

hell with it and touching him again. But the stiff way he held himself was reminder enough that their whole dynamic had just shifted.

He picked up her underwear and held it out, still without looking at her. She snatched it out of his hand, but going through the motions of putting them back on was beyond her right now.

Avery wrapped her arms around herself. No. Their dynamic hadn't shifted. It was just sex. Outstanding sex, sure, but still just sex. Drew had more than proved himself capable of having no-strings-attached sex with anyone who came along. Nothing had to change between them. They wouldn't lose their friendship over this.

She hoped.

He fished his keys out of his pocket, hesitated like he was going to say something, and then seemed to decide against it. Without another word, he turned around and walked out of the kitchen.

She didn't take a full breath until she heard her front door shut. Then Avery scrambled to get dressed. "What the hell was I thinking?"

That one was easy—she hadn't been. As soon as he kissed her, all rational thought cruised right out the window. And look at her now, standing in the middle of her kitchen, dangerously close to a mental breakdown. She turned around, wishing the answer would burst from the walls and hit her in the face. Or maybe her sink would spring a leak, and she'd be forced to deal with just about anything other than the thoughts circling in her head.

Her gaze landed on her phone where it had fallen to the floor in the middle of…all that. *The phone. That's the answer.*

She just needed someone to talk her down from the ledge she stood on—someone with ovaries.

Bri.

Avery practically dove for the phone and clicked through to dial her friend. Even hearing the ring was enough to calm her down a little. This wasn't the end of the world. Sure, she'd had sex with Drew, but that didn't mean she had to freak out about it. She was an adult, owner of her sexuality, and what was more, it wasn't sex for the sake of sex. The endgame was all that mattered—a baby. She could do this to have a baby.

God, she hoped she could do this.

• • •

Drew's phone went off before his alarm. He groaned and rolled over, peeling his eyes open to see that it was barely 7 a.m. "Why, God, why?" His phone rang again, the obnoxious tone one he'd picked out solely because he'd always hear it, no matter what he was doing.

There was no ignoring that shit.

With a curse, he groped for it on the nightstand and answered without looking at the screen. "Flannery."

"Are you fucking insane?"

He winced and held the phone away from his ear. "Hey, Ryan. Nice of you to call at the ass crack of dawn."

"What were you thinking?" His brother didn't pause to let him answer. "No, I know exactly what you were thinking. You can't stand the thought of Avery being with another guy—which is *not* what she was planning to do, by the way."

His brain finally caught up with what had Ryan so pissed. Drew sat up and rubbed a hand over his face. "It has nothing to do with that. I'm being a good friend."

"A good friend would offer to hold her hand, *not* be her sperm donor."

"Jesus, just calm down. Avery is fine with it, so why are your panties in such a twist?"

"*Because* it's Avery. You ever stop to think about the future? Are you going to stop hanging out with her all the time?"

"Of course not. Nothing's going to change." He climbed out of bed and went in search of clothes.

Ryan laughed. "God, you're delusional. Nothing's going to change? You're having fucking sex with the goal of making a baby together and you're not *together*. How confusing is that going to be for the kid? Hell, forget the kid. How much is seeing that kid grow up going to mess with *you*?"

It was one thing he hadn't spent too much time thinking about in the last twenty-four hours. He'd be there for Avery, but he wasn't going to be a father, not like Billy had been. It'd be more like a favorite uncle, always around to help out, without any of the soul-crushing shit. "Jesus, Ryan, let it go. How did you even find out about it?"

"You're an idiot. Women talk, and apparently she was shaken up when she called Bri."

His heart stopped. Things hadn't been ideal with how he left yesterday, but Avery couldn't have been clearer about her desire to get him the hell out of her house. He'd thought it was just post-sex awkwardness—or that's what he told himself when he leapt at the excuse to get the hell out of there before he did something crazy like drag her to bed. But if he'd left and she wasn't okay… Fuck, he was a special kind of shithead. "Is she hurt?"

"You are so far off the point, it's not even funny. She's fine—for now."

Drew pulled on a pair of jeans and hooked his shirt off the dresser. It was early, but maybe he'd drop by to make sure Avery really *was* okay. Then his brother's words registered. "For now? What are you talking about?"

"Dude, you guys are closer than most married couples I know. Or you were before you decided to go and fuck with it."

Something in his chest twisted viciously at the thought of losing Avery. It wasn't something he let himself think about often, because even the threat of it was enough to open up a pit inside him that he wasn't sure there was a cure for. But it was manageable—as long as their friendship stayed in the boundaries they had set up.

Except he'd gone and changed that yesterday.

"Nothing's going to change," he repeated, as much to reassure himself as his brother. "It's just sex."

"Except it isn't. The only time sex without strings works—and you already know what I think of that shit—is when you aren't already in love with the woman before you go there."

"You make it sound like I've been holding a torch for her." When his brother didn't immediately say anything, he nearly threw his phone out the window to just get away from the damn conversation. "I haven't."

"Yeah, sure. You've loved her since you were like six."

He scrubbed the back of his hand over his mouth. "Of course I have. The same way you'd love a sister or something."

"A sister you want to sleep with?"

"For fuck's sake, that was a bad comparison. It's strictly platonic." Except for all the times he'd had to remind himself that Avery was off-limits.

"Maybe it was, but sex changes everything — not to mention a goddamn baby. If you don't know that, then you're an even bigger idiot than I'd have guessed."

He didn't want to talk about this right now. "Things are going just fine. Avery's fine. I'm fine."

Ryan huffed out a breath. "Whatever you have to tell yourself."

"When did you turn into such a dick?"

"I don't know. Maybe when you and Avery came up with the plan to strand me and Bri in a fucking cabin for three days."

He had to admit, it was one of their more brilliant ideas. "Yeah, and look how that worked out." It didn't matter how many times they pointed out the end result, Ryan and Bri just wouldn't let it go.

"Just because one insane scheme of yours worked out doesn't mean the rest of them will — and there's more at stake with this one than either of you seem to realize."

"Okay, Dr. Phil." He glanced at the clock. "I have to go. I need to run into Williamsport for a bit this afternoon."

"That's right. Run away from the conversation. I'm sure that will solve everything."

The statement hit a little too close to home. Giving Avery her space yesterday wasn't running — it was being prudent, damn it. "I do have a job that needs my attention."

Ryan laughed. "As one runner to another, I say *bullshit*. I'm way better at it than you are. But do what you have to do."

"And with that glowing endorsement, I'm going."

"Wait!"

Christ, would it never end? He closed his eyes and strove

for patience. "What?"

"As fun as this conversation's been, it's not why I called. Bri wants you and Avery to babysit Friday. You know, if you're not too busy banging your best friend."

"Why do you need both of us?" Avery was more than capable of taking care of Lily on her own.

"You're the one trying to procreate right now. We figure you need the practice."

"We'll be there." Even if it was so he could smack some sense into his idiot younger brother. He hung up without saying goodbye, more rattled than he wanted to admit. It'd be a lot easier to shove off his brother's comments if he didn't already feel like he was on a slippery slope.

The problem was, he couldn't exactly talk to Avery about it. Drew could just picture that conversation.

So, this isn't really working out for me because now I'm seeing you as more than a best friend, and that's after only having sex once. I value our friendship too highly to risk it. Do I want to stop having sex? Hell no. Yesterday was better than I could have imagined and I sure as fuck don't plan on giving that up until I have to.

Yeah, that'd really go over well.

But he couldn't get Ryan's words out of his head.

Whatever his brother thought, he wasn't an idiot. He *knew* he could lose Avery. It was something that over the years he'd lost more sleep thinking about than he'd ever admit. There were so many things that could take her away from him, from the cancer that plagued her family, to another man. But he'd been able to brush off those possibilities when they were just that—possibilities.

Now he was staring that risk in the face, and it was his

own doing.

Drew rubbed his chest. He'd seen what loss like that could do to a Flannery man. He was too young to remember exactly what his parents' marriage was like, but one time Miss Nora at the library had told him that she'd never seen a love like the one between his father and mother. It was enough to push his old man past the point of no return after she died. Christ, hadn't his dad kept a goddamn shrine to her all those years? It was the only part of their house that wasn't mired in filth.

And that wasn't even getting into the raggedy stuffed teddy bear Drew had found in his old man's bed when he cleaned the house out after his death—the one with the inscription on its belly that read, *To the love of my life.*

No, he never wanted to experience a love like that.

He walked into the kitchen and poured himself a glass of orange juice, wishing he could drown out those memories. It didn't matter what had happened to his old man, because his bond with Avery was different. She was his best friend—not the love of his life.

That said, he couldn't lose her.

Which meant he had to figure out a way to keep her from overthinking this thing. As long as they kept it simple, there was no reason for it to change anything between them. This wasn't forever. Once she was knocked up, things would go back to normal.

A new memory arose, one from yesterday, when he'd been buried inside her and feeling her come around his cock. She hadn't been overthinking shit then. Drew grinned. Yeah, he knew just the way to drive these worries out of both their minds.

And fuck if that didn't brighten his day.

Chapter Seven

Avery parked in the tiny lot behind her store and let herself in the back, leaving the door unlocked for her sister. Alexis had promised to meet her there and walk down to the Diner for breakfast, but she'd shown up early to give herself some time to settle her thoughts. Even talking with Bri last night hadn't been enough to completely erase her worry that this sex thing was going to ruin her friendship with Drew.

And now she had to break the news to her sister.

She stood just inside the doorway to the main floor and took a deep breath, letting the faint smell of age roll over her. Stepping into her antique shop was always a relief. There was so much history there, each piece she bought with its own story to tell, to the point where Bri had always joked that the shop was her version of a library. Avery mostly just liked the sense of past and future she felt. She was just the person holding these things between one owner and the next, but as soon as the items entered her shop, she became part of their history.

It was a heady thing.

While she waited for Alexis, she went to work cutting the newest additions out of their boxes and bubble wrap. One was a Victorian rocking chair that desperately needed a new set of cushions, and the other was an old baby buggy with giant wheels and a great arching handle.

"That looks like something from *Rosemary's Baby*."

She jumped, hating the guilt that flared when she saw her sister. "God, you're quieter than a cat."

Alexis slid between a giant bookshelf filled with first editions and the rocking chair. "Lots of practice dealing with families who don't want to be disturbed." She made a face. "I prefer the maternity ward. The parents tend to be happy, and the babies' needs are simple enough."

Which made the news about her plan that much harder to share. God, she wasn't ready to deal with hurting her sister like this.

Alexis pulled up a chair and carefully lowered herself into it. The thing was so sturdy, she and three of her closest friends could have danced on it, but Avery didn't bother correcting her. Her sister leaned forward and peered at the buggy. "So what's the deal? I thought you said something about spending the morning with Drew. He's not hiding in that armoire again, is he? That ass scared the crap out of me last time."

"He's not here." The whole banging-on-her-kitchen-counter had changed the plans they made last week. "Something came up." Mainly him, yesterday.

"It always does." When Avery sent her a look, she held up her hands. "What? You know I'm right. Mr. Footloose and Fancy-free? Drew isn't exactly known for his stability."

Maybe not to the rest of the world, but he'd always been there for her. She wished she could say he'd grown up in recent years, now that he'd reached the magical age of thirty, but it wouldn't be the full truth. He'd slowed down, but there was no changing his ways. Drew was never going to settle down.

Not that she was holding out for him or something. Because that would be crazy. She carefully pulled at the piece of foam covering the carriage wheel closest to her. "He has his moments."

"I won't argue that." A shadow passed over Alexis's face, and she knew they were both thinking back to how vital the Flannery brothers had been when their mother died. They were barely more than kids at the time, but Drew, especially, had stepped up to the plate and helped her and Alexis escape during the times when it all became too much. Dad hadn't checked out on them the way Billy Flannery had on his boys, but she didn't know if she would have gotten through it without Drew next to her.

They'd been close before her mother died, but afterward they were inseparable. Out of all her friends, he alone knew what it was like to grow up without a mom. And he never held it against her when she broke down, the strain of being strong too much sometimes.

It was now or never. If she let this go on too long, she'd do something—anything—besides telling her sister the truth. Avery wadded up the garbage and dumped it into the cardboard box next to her. "There is something I wanted to talk to you about—and Drew's involved."

Alexis's hazel eyes went wide. "Holy crap, are you two

finally dating?"

All her plans and stress about how to approach this with her sister flew right out of her head. "What?"

"Well, you know we've all been wondering when you two would see the light of day and realize you're perfect for each other. I'm so glad you finally have, because I was starting to get worried."

"Alexis, we're best friends."

Her sister raised her eyebrows. "What's your point?"

"That's just…" She started to say Drew was more a brother than anything else, but the words died before she gave them voice. Even if he had been before—and that was debatable—he sure as hell wasn't now that she'd had him inside her. "I know everything about him. Twenty years is a lot of history to suddenly turn into romance."

"And what's so bad about you being best friends? There's a kind of trust that comes from that much history, that you can't find with most other people." She made a face. "If you were together *he* wouldn't dump you a month before your wedding."

Like Alexis's fiancé had done, when he'd decided she'd recovered enough from her emergency hysterectomy to be able to handle the news that he didn't want to be married to a barren woman. To this day, if Avery ever met him on a deserted street, she would have no problem running Eric's bitch ass over. But her sister was strong. She'd picked up the pieces and moved on with her life. Mostly.

Avery worried her news was going to throw the past in her sister's face.

"This isn't about me and Drew suddenly going into freakishly romantic territory." Getting naked in the name of making a baby certainly didn't count. "It's about a decision I made that he's supporting me in."

God, this was so much harder than she expected.

Alexis leaned forward to prop her elbows on her thighs, appearing to give Avery her full attention. "Whatever it is, you can tell me."

Of course her big sister would offer unconditional support without ever bothering to question what it was in support of. Avery almost chickened out right then and there. She cleared her suddenly dry throat. "I'm going to have a baby."

For one terrifying moment, Alexis's face was perfectly blank. "A baby?"

It was too late to turn back now that the cat was out of the bag. "Yeah."

"You're having a baby…right now." Every word out of her mouth was as empty as the expression on her face.

"I don't know if it's *right now*, but I'm trying." She bit her lip to keep from babbling, because that would only make this worse.

"This is…surprising." Her sister's eyes shone. "I can't believe it."

And she still didn't know if that was good surprise or bad surprise coming from Alexis. "I…" Her determination not to babble evaporated. "I'm okay with adopting later, but after what happened with Mom, and then you…and the doctor told me it's only a matter of time before I have to take the same steps you did. Am I a selfish bitch for doing this? Maybe I should just adopt and count myself lucky to be alive."

"Avery, calm down." Alexis finally straightened. Her

chin trembled for a moment, the only indication Avery's words had cut her deeply. "You don't have to make a huge life decision like this based on how I'd feel about it."

That was the thing. As much as she wasn't going to change her mind, she hated the thought of causing her sister any kind of pain. The blank expression was back in place, and while her sister was clearly throwing her a bone, keeping her answers and her expression devoid of emotion, she'd be a *really* selfish bitch to accept it. "Tell me the truth, Alexis. How *do* you feel about it?"

Several seconds passed before Alexis said, "I… I'll be okay." She squeezed Avery's hands again, and even managed a smile. "Really, I will."

"Alexis…" God, she'd screwed up. It was written all over her sister's face. Maybe someone who didn't know her wouldn't notice, but Avery knew better.

"If this is something you've thought through — and, despite your current freakout, I think you have — then I fully support you."

Of course she did. Avery's shoulders slumped. *I am the worst sister ever.* "I'm sorry. I never meant to hurt you." It was the last thing in the world she wanted.

"You can't put your life on hold just to save me from pain." Her voice went fierce. "Don't you *dare* put your life on hold for someone else — even me. You deserve better than that." She pushed to her feet before Avery could get a word out. "How about breakfast?"

It couldn't be more obvious that her sister wanted to get out of there and away from their discussion. Avery nodded and followed her to the back door. They walked in silence around the side of the building and down the sidewalk toward the Diner. Even at the early weekday hour, the street was plenty busy, and the early spring weather had people sharing her need to walk and enjoy it.

Too bad she wasn't enjoying much right now, not with guilt making each breath she inhaled feel like blades in her throat. She let Alexis lead the way into the diner. The faint grease smell made her smile, despite the circumstances. This place was a staple of her high school years, and she loved how little it had changed since then. She was pretty sure the cracked red vinyl seats were the same ones they'd put in when they built this place, and the familiar black and white tiled floor was the same that graced diners across the country.

The waitress, Dorothy, walked over, eyeing them as if she expected trouble. "Alexis. Avery. Just two?"

"Yep." Avery slid into the booth and waited for the woman to shuffle away before she leaned across the table and whispered, "You know, I don't think she's forgiven me for Matt Jennings."

Alexis smiled. "That was ten years ago."

"And yet I can still remember the look on his face perfectly." Specifically, the way his smirk turned into actual fear when he realized she wasn't going to back down after she hit him the first time. "Think that makes me a bad person?"

"I don't know. Do you still think about punching him in the face and wish you could do it again?"

"Nah. He deserved that one, but he shaped up after that." Probably because she'd threatened his life if he ever called her sister a prude cunt again. She was nearly one hundred percent certain that Drew had made the same threat, but she'd never been able to confirm it.

Alexis shook her head. "Did I ever tell you thank you for standing up for my honor like that?"

"You didn't have to. You're my sister."

Dorothy approached and slid two glasses of water in front of them. "Since you won't be assaulting anyone today, what'll you have?"

So much for Dorothy forgiving and forgetting.

They ordered and watched her walk away. Alexis turned to face Avery. "I'm sure you've thought about this, but *Nâi-nai* and *Yé-ye* are going to flip if you pick a donor that's not fully Chinese."

A fact she knew all too well, especially considering who she'd chosen. "It's Drew."

"I'm sorry, what?" Alexis shook her head as if trying to dislodge something from her ear. "I thought you just said Drew is the sperm donor."

Now probably wasn't the best time to admit they were going about things the old-fashioned way. *Never* sounded like a much better schedule. "He is."

She opened her mouth, shut it, and then opened it again. "I can think of half a dozen ways that will bite you in the ass later on, but I'm sure you've thought of the same things."

More or less. She was hanging onto the endgame like a lifeline. "If it has to be someone, I'm glad it's him."

That, at least, was the truth. It didn't matter what new trials she would go through because of this crazy plan, she found a strange comfort in the fact she would be going through them with Drew, even if he didn't have the same level of long-term commitment she did when it came to the baby.

"As long as you're sure this won't blow up in your face."

Avery laughed. "I'm pretty sure it's *guaranteed* to blow up in my face. But it's worth it."

"Then I'm happy for you."

She wasn't sure if she really believed Alexis, or if it was just her own issues getting in the way and making her project her feelings onto her sister. "Thank you."

Alexis sat back as Dorothy brought their food, depositing it with a sniff. "I always wanted to be an Auntie."

"You'll be the best there is." Oh crap, now she was going to cry. She tried to cover up a sniffle with a cough and grabbed a fork to dig into her omelet. Stuffing her face was just the distraction she needed.

Alexis poked at her hashbrowns. "So... When are you going to tell the rest of the family?"

The eggs in her mouth suddenly felt a whole lot chewier. She swallowed with difficulty. "Um... Ten months from now?"

Alexis finally smiled. "I'm not going to lie, there's a petty part of me that's looking forward to seeing the look on *Yéye*'s face when you deliver the news."

"Gee, thanks."

Her sister shrugged. "I tried to do things their way. Eric was the only guy I ever dated who they approved of, and look how that turned out." She toasted Avery with her water. "I thought I was destined to be the greatest disappointment of their life and now you're off to get knocked up out of wedlock by a white guy."

"I do nothing halfway." And, if her doing this took some of the pressure off her sister, she was okay with that, too. But all through the rest of breakfast, she couldn't shake the feeling that she was dealing her sister a heart wound Alexis might not recover from. It *had* to be projection—Alexis chatted away about her job at the hospital and didn't bring up the baby again. Like nothing was wrong.

All the while, the weight on Avery's shoulders got heavier and heavier. By the time they made it back to her shop and said their goodbyes, she was surprised she wasn't crawling under it. Even unpacking the rest of the baby buggy wasn't enough to shake the feeling.

She leaned against the front desk and stared at her phone. The sad truth was that there was only one person who could make her feel better about this, and he was the one person she wasn't sure she could call right now.

No, that was bullshit. Maybe he was in the same boat as she was, wondering if yesterday was a mistake, but she'd never know unless she reached out. Hell, it was just one time. If they decided not to do it again, then at least she'd *know*. This gray area where she didn't know if they were okay was killing her as much as her guilt about Alexis.

All she had to do was pick up the phone and make the call.

Well, she refused to be a coward, and there was never a better time than now. She dialed, hating herself for holding her breath, and nearly hung up in a panic when he answered, "Flannery."

Her nervous energy got away from her, and words popped out of her mouth before she could think better of them. "Morning! Just calling with your daily sex status report."

A heartbeat, and then he laughed. "Okay, I'll bite. How'd I do?"

"Oh, you know, just fine."

"Fine?" A car door slammed somewhere in the distance. "Sweetheart, that was a far sight better than 'fine.'"

She was going to get through this with sheer bravado. The only other option was to sit down and talk about their feelings, which *so* wasn't on the menu if Avery had anything to say about it. A little more relaxed now, she settled onto the rocking chair and propped her feet on the chest. "It was a solid six."

"That's so cute when you mix up your numbers. Yesterday was a ten."

She paused, pretending to consider. "Oh, no, definitely not a ten. I would have noticed if Sam Elliott or Sean Connery showed up."

"You have seriously questionable taste."

"I do not. I have excellent taste. Those voices…" She sighed, putting a little extra breathiness into it. "Actually, I'm adding Benedict Cumberbatch to that list. He'd be a ten."

"No. Absolutely not. I draw the line at being outranked by a man with better cheekbones than most women. He is *not* attractive."

"Don't be jealous that you can't make women come just by talking to them."

"Two words—phone sex."

Her laugh died. After what they'd just done, she didn't like the reminder that he'd rocked other women's worlds, but she'd better get used to it. This was Drew, and he'd never had a problem with the ladies. "Kudos to you, then."

His tone shifted, the playfulness disappearing. "What are you doing for lunch?"

You. No, wait, she couldn't say that. She still didn't know where they stood. She couldn't just assume they were going to keep having sex because they were joking about yesterday. Avery twisted her hair. "I hadn't decided."

"I'll make it easy on you—my place, noon."

The growl in his voice made her shiver, but she forced a laugh. "Are we going to walk twenty paces and have a shootout?"

"If by shootout, you mean you're going to come screaming my name, then yes. See you then." She hoped he'd hung up before he heard her whimper.

Holy shit.

Avery set her phone down, trying to ignore the way her hand shook. "Well, I guess that answers that."

Chapter Eight

Drew hissed out a breath as he turned his police cruiser onto Main Street, all the good feelings from his conversation with Avery disappearing in the face of the call he'd just gotten. Rusty, drunk and making a scene. Again.

He was completely unsurprised to find Gena standing outside Chilly's front door as he pulled up. She shifted from one foot to the other, her expression worried. He took another breath and put on his professional mask—the one that showed nothing—and climbed out into the brisk spring morning.

The parking lot was mostly deserted, which wasn't unexpected considering noon was still a while off. Gena tried for a smile as he walked up. "Sorry for this. It's just worse than normal and Old Joe can't carry him alone."

No, Old Joe wouldn't be able to haul Rusty's drunk ass anywhere. The middle-aged man had to be well over two-fifty, and Joe's back wasn't as good as it used to be. It was why he'd retired from the old mill a few years ago. Drew nodded. "I'll take care of it."

"Thank you." Her smile was a little wilted around the edges, but she brightened it up a notch or two as she looked up at him.

It brought to mind the look on Avery's face yesterday. He shook his head. Now wasn't the time to get distracted with the memories that had stolen more than their fair share of sleep in the dark hours of the morning. He slid past Gena and into Chilly's dim hallway.

The quiet raised the small hairs on the back of his neck. He usually tried to stop in there a few times a week and have a beer. With the after-work crowd around, it was a good way to take the pulse of the town and head off any potential problems at the pass.

This was different. The only times he'd been there this early in the past were because his old man, Billy, liked to start early. Some days he could keep it going until he found his way home, but the bad days ended like this—with the sheriff hauling his drunk ass home.

Those were the days Drew made up some excuse to get Ryan out of the house for the few hours it would take Billy to pass out. It was bad enough that he had to clean up after the man when he was too boozed up to do it himself. He didn't want his little brother to see that, too.

But this wasn't his father causing problems now, not with Billy nine years in the grave. No, it was Rusty, who seemed all too eager to take over the position as the town drunk.

Drew paused in the doorway and caught Old Joe's eye. The relief on the man's face let him know just how bad things had gotten. Rusty was slumped in his stool, his heavy body propped up on the bar—the only thing keeping him from falling on his ass. He lifted his head off his arms and blinked. "Sheriff?" He turned to Joe. "Why'd yous have to call the Sheriff? I'm s'fine."

"Sure you are, Rusty. Fine and dandy." Joe met Drew halfway across the bar. "He's been going on about his girls again."

'His girls' being the daughters he lost all rights to when his marriage ended a few years ago. By this point, all of Wellingford knew the truth—he was in a situation of his own making—but to hear Rusty tell it, his bitch of an ex-wife slept with the judge, the lawyer, and anyone else it took, in order to get his custody taken away. If he was ranting about that again, he was in it in a bad way. The only help for it was to get him home as quickly as possible.

He moved past Joe. "I got it."

"You sure? No shame in asking for help."

It was the same thing Old Joe had said to him when he was thirteen and had been caught stealing cans of ravioli from the grocery store. Joe paid for the food and sat him down to explain that he couldn't be expected to shoulder every burden alone. Drew had stammered and been embarrassed and claimed up one side and down the other that he and Ryan were fine, but every week after that, groceries started appearing in their pantry. God knew it hadn't come from Billy, so there was only one person who could have done it.

He forced a smile. "I'm sure. Just going to get him home and head back to the station."

Joe held his gaze for a few moments while Rusty muttered something indecipherable, and then he nodded.

"You know where to find me if you change your mind."

"Yep." He stepped around the old man and muscled Rusty off the barstool. "Come on, buddy. We're going to get you home." Though it'd serve him right if Drew dumped him in one of the two cells at the station and forced him to sleep it off there.

He could feel the eyes of the few people in Chilly's on him as he stumbled out the front door, half-carrying Rusty alongside him. The stale alcohol stench stuck in Drew's throat, but he made himself keep breathing and fight back the memories it brought with it. He was a grown man now. He wasn't a little boy, terrified and in over his head. That was ancient history.

It didn't feel that way, though, as he drove through town, taking the same path he'd driven over the last few years more times than he could count. Rusty's house didn't look much like the one Drew grew up in, but it had the same neglected air.

The judge had good reason for denying custody.

Ten minutes later, he had Rusty in bed, facedown to avoid any choking issues, with a glass of water and a bucket next to the bed. He made himself take one last look. The empty bottles around the bed were all too familiar. Hell, everything about this room was. The only difference was the man on the bed. Where Rusty was bloated by his drinking, Billy had whittled himself down to practically nothing.

His first breath outside the house wasn't nearly cleansing enough. He was sure he could still smell the liquor seeping from Rusty's pores. Christ, he needed a shower.

He glanced at his watch. Getting the drunk home had taken longer than he expected, and he was damn near late for his meeting with Avery. Again. He hustled to his cruiser and made a quick call to the station to tell them he was taking a long lunch before he came back for the evening shift. Working doubles was a bitch, but one of his deputies was out with the flu, so he didn't have a choice.

The drive west out of town was one he'd done so many times, he let his mind wander as he took the road's curves through the trees, needing to think of anything but the town drunk—either past or present.

Unsurprisingly, his mind wandered right over to Avery.

He grinned as he thought back over their conversation. After talking with Ryan, he'd been worried that she was all torn up over this thing—he'd actually been about to call her when she beat him to it. But she'd joked and laughed and sounded perfectly normal.

Obviously his brother was overreacting. She was just fine.

As if she'd been drawn into existence by his thinking about her, he caught sight of the Beast about a quarter mile in front of him.

A fucking ridiculous idea took root—the perfect distraction from the old nightmare at Chilly's, and the equally perfect way to teach her a lesson—just the kind of thing they'd always done. It was a risk, but one he deemed worthwhile. He flipped on his lights and siren. They'd see if she'd give him a goddamn six after this.

In a matter of seconds, the cruiser was riding up her ass, and it was another thirty seconds before she pulled over onto a little dirt road, driving until the trees closed in around them, shielding both their vehicles from the main road. Fighting back a grin, he put on his hat and sunglasses.

This was going to be exactly what he needed.

• • •

Avery watched him climb out of his cruiser, wondering what the hell he was up to now. She had to admit Drew cut a delicious figure in his uniform, with his hat pulled low and aviator sunglasses shielding his eyes. As she waited, he skirted the trees stretching over the dirt road and stopped next to her car.

He made a circling motion for her to put down her window, and she rolled her eyes. It was a crapshoot, when he got like this, whether he was going to pull some act straight out of *Super Troopers*—because God knew he found the whole meow joke *hilarious*—or actually give her a ticket, like he had last time. Her insurance would go up if she got another one, so he'd better throw that idea right out the window. If he did that, baby or not, he *so* wasn't getting laid. "Yes, officer?"

"Do you know how fast you were driving?"

Wow, he was really going there? She debated making a run for it, but he was parked behind her. Besides, they were supposed to meet for midday nookie, and there wouldn't be another opportunity today. So she pressed her lips together and tried to keep a hold of her temper. "Are you serious?"

"Ma'am, I asked you a question."

Obviously he wasn't going to deviate from his little game, so she might as well play along. "Yeah, I was speeding. I have this hot date, you see. My best friend is about to bang my brains out and I'm kind of in a hurry to make that happen."

The muscle ticking in his jaw was the only indication what she'd said affected him. "There's no need for that kind of attitude, ma'am."

Avery stared at her reflection in his sunglasses. She'd actually dressed up today, to the point where she'd left the sweats at home, choosing instead to throw on a jean skirt she hadn't even known she had, and a black tank top. She'd even kept her hair down, which she never did because it always ended up in her face. And here he was, fucking with her—and not in the way she wanted. "Let me just grab my baseball bat and I'll show you attitude."

No change in expression. "Ma'am, will you step out of the vehicle?"

Oh, she'd step out of the vehicle all right. She was going to whoop his ass. Avery gave him her sweetest smile. "Sure thing." She threw open the door, forcing him to back up to avoid being taken out. From there, she hopped to the ground, since there was no graceful way to climb out of her Jeep in a mini skirt, and she wasn't feeling generous enough to flash him when he was acting like a dick.

His mouth tightened and his chin dipped, as if he was taking her in. "What the fuck are you wearing?"

She looked at herself. Apparently she was out of line for putting a little effort into her appearance. "God, *fine*. Forget it happened. I think I have some jeans in the back."

"I don't think so." He reached for his side, pulling out a pair of handcuffs. "Turn around."

"No way." A ticket was one thing, but the cuffs were something else altogether. With her luck, he'd toss her into the back of his cruiser just for the hell of it. "Knock it off, Drew. Let's just go to your place and get this over with." Because this little joke was putting a damper on her desire to get naked and sweaty with him.

He grabbed her arm and spun her around, using a hand at the back of her neck to bend her over the hood of her Jeep. It was obviously a move he'd done quite a bit, because it happened so fast she didn't have time to react. Between one blink and the next, he had her wrists cuffed behind her. The position made her skirt ride up until she was pretty sure the bottom of her ass was hanging out. "Hey!"

He leaned over her, covering her with his body, and she stopped struggling at the feel of the hard length of him pressed against her backside. *Whoa.* Where had that come from? She swallowed, trying to process the one-eighty her hormones did, from anger to desire, in a single beat of her heart.

It was because she wanted the end result of this—the baby—not because being at his mercy and having his hands on her got her hot. "Is that a baton in your pocket, officer, or are you just happy to see me?"

"Oh, sweetheart, I'm definitely happy to see you." He straightened, leaving her feeling even more exposed than she had to begin with, because now she was missing the heat of his body. He cursed.

What was the problem? She bit back the question. It didn't really matter. All that mattered was that he kept touching her. He ran his hands down her spine, stopping just before reaching the cuffs. Then he pulled her into a standing position, using his hips to keep her pinned against the side of the Jeep, and repeated the process with the front of her body.

Or he started to. It stopped being a cursory exploration as soon as he reached her breasts. He cupped her, squeezing. "Why the hell aren't you wearing a bra?"

He lightly pinched her nipples and she shivered. "I wasn't aware I was talking to the fashion police."

"Do you know what it does to me knowing you're driving around, a short step away from being topless?" His breath brushed the back of her neck and over one shoulder, raising goose bumps in its wake.

Probably the same thing it did to Avery. She didn't make a habit of going braless, but she might start if *this* was the reaction she got. She took a shaky breath. "Then I guess you better not do a panty check."

Drew froze for one eternal second. Then he pushed her back down over the hood of her Jeep and dragged her skirt up to bunch around her hips. A breeze chose that moment to hit—as if she needed the reminder of just how exposed she was. But then he slid a hand between her legs, and she didn't care much about anything else at all.

"You're already wet." He teased her, fingers brushing her clit, her entrance, and back again, nothing close to what she needed. "I think you like it when I toss you around."

She gritted her teeth, fighting against the need to spread her legs to give him better access, and beg for him to just *touch* her. "Nah. I was touching myself while I was driving."

"Really?" He kept up his maddening route. "And what were you thinking about?"

Hell, if she actually had started early, she'd have been thinking about *him*. Yesterday had given her plenty of ammunition for fantasies. No way in hell would she admit as much, though. "Sean Connery. Obviously."

"Obviously." His laugh was a little harsh. "Guess I'll have to up my game if I want you in the here and now, huh?"

Up his game? Only if he wanted to kill her. Avery

couldn't admit she was so affected. She wouldn't. It was just sex—and sex with a deadline, at that. She let her cheek rest against the cool metal of the hood, striving for control. "I don't know. Sean Connery is a pretty tough act to follow."

"Sean Connery, huh?"

"Yep." She was lying through her teeth and she had a pretty good idea that he knew it. His fingers pushed deeper, spreading her until she couldn't help but rock against him. She gritted her teeth. "He was really good."

"I bet." His lips found the back of her neck. "It's a shame you have to settle for me."

The ass didn't sound the least bit bothered by it, either. She hissed out a breath at the feeling of his palm cupping her. Owning her. It wasn't supposed to be this intense. She closed her eyes, but that only made it worse, because she couldn't pretend she was with anyone else but Drew.

She didn't want to.

He turned her around and pressed her back against the Beast. "Open your eyes."

Helpless to do anything else, she obeyed. The look on his face nearly stopped her heart, as if he was searching her expression for something she wasn't sure she wanted to give him. As if he saw *everything*. "Drew—"

"Shut up." He yanked her shirt up and over her head, and then pulled it down her arms to tangle with the cuffs. His gaze dropped to her breasts, releasing her, but it didn't feel like release as he dipped down and took one nipple in his mouth. There was nothing tender or soft about the motion— he sucked hard, setting his teeth against her sensitive flesh, just this side of hurting her.

She gasped and arched up, offering him more as he

moved to the other nipple. What this man could do with his mouth was out of this world. It was all too easy to remember exactly what he'd done to her yesterday after he kissed down her stomach, and the memory only heightened what they were currently doing.

He lifted her onto the hood of her Jeep and spread her legs. Which was right about the time that she realized exactly how naked she was, and just how close to a public street *they* were. He followed her look and gripped her chin, guiding her face back to his. "I won't let anyone see."

How the hell was he going to *stop* someone from seeing? And he was in his freaking cruiser. "You're going to get fired."

"Sweetheart, no one uses this road outside of deer season. You're safe with me. I promise."

He said it with such confidence, she couldn't doubt him. Or maybe she was just beyond caring right now. She started to reach for him but came up short when the move pulled on the cuffs. "I want to touch you."

"I'm about to do enough touching for the both of us." He kissed her, his tongue demanding she open for him. She heard the faint sound of a zipper and then his cock was there, tracing her entrance and spreading her wetness around. Avery tried to pull back so she could look, but he kept her pinned with his body and a hand on the back of her neck.

His mouth plundered hers as he sank into her, inch by decadent inch. The dual sensations sent her head spinning, only made stronger by the fact she couldn't do more than rock against him, sliding him a little bit deeper.

He broke the kiss and leaned back, his hands going to her thighs and spreading her even wider. "Now, you can watch me fucking you."

Finally, *finally* she could see him slide in and out of her, and damn if the sight didn't push her that much closer to the edge. She whimpered.

"Say my name. Now, Avery." He let go of one thigh without breaking his rhythm, and hooked the back of her neck again, forcing her face up to his, kissably close. "I want my name on your lips as you come."

No. She'd already given him more than she could have anticipated. She'd be damned before she gave him *that*, too. He slammed into her, the harshness of the move enough to send her hurtling into orgasm. She closed her eyes and screamed, but not loud enough to drown out his curse. It didn't matter. He let go of her neck and pushed her down to lie on the hood, using the new position to pound into her, finishing with another muted curse.

Even knowing she should get up or cover herself or something, she couldn't do more than lie there and breathe. "Best. Non-ticket. Ever."

"Glad you think so." He stroked her clit, making her squirm. "Avery, look at me."

She bit her lip and opened her eyes to find him propping himself up against the Jeep. This was where he'd pull out of her and yank up his pants and things would get strange. She took a breath, bracing for the weird.

But Drew just gave her a wicked grin, the heat in his blue eyes completely undimmed by what they'd just done. "Next time, we're making it to a bed. And you'll be screaming my name so many times, you'll be hoarse for days afterward."

Oh. My. God.

Chapter Nine

Avery paced in front of her closet for the seventh time, her towel still wrapped around her from the earlier shower. Getting ready would be a hell of a lot easier if she hadn't had Drew's words circling in her head for the last twenty-four hours. *A bed*. It shouldn't be that startling. They had only had sex twice, so it made sense that they'd end up in a bed at some point before her fertile time was up. But…he'd said it with such purpose—with such *promise*.

Now it was all she could think about.

It didn't help that she had nothing to wear, which had never been a problem until right this second. Jeans and T-shirts were her gig and she was totally okay with that—comfort was king. Not to mention, they were going to babysit. How pathetic was it that she was sitting here debating clothing choices for *that?*

But here she was, sporting makeup for the first time since Bri had that fundraiser for the library six months ago, her hair down instead of in a ponytail, and actually putting thought into what she should wear.

This so wasn't her.

It shouldn't matter if tonight ended with epic sex or not. She was still *Avery* and she didn't obsess about stuff like this. Angry at herself—and at Drew for being the one to spark this change in perspective—she pulled on her favorite cutoff shorts and a black T-shirt. Simple. Like she hadn't just spent fifteen minutes agonizing over clothes.

Everything about this situation was spiraling out of control. She had Drew acting like… She wasn't even sure how to define it—or whether it was all in her head or he really *was* acting kind of weird. Maybe she was imagining that possessive edge, or maybe that was just how he acted when he was banging someone. It wasn't like she'd know, after all.

She strode into her kitchen and looked around. He wouldn't be there for a bit, and she was going to go crazy if she didn't keep her hands busy. If she kept moving, hopefully it would be enough to beat back all her issues.

Yeah, right. She hurried around the living room, picking up a scattering of gamer magazines and tossing them into the basket at the end of the couch. Last time Drew was there, he'd paged through damn near every single one in a quest to find the tiny article about the upcoming Call of Duty game. She'd laughed at him the entire time.

She stopped short, staring at the cover of *OXM*. If this thing blew up in her face, she'd lose that. There would be no more dropping in for silly reasons. Hell, there might not be any dropping in *at all*.

Rationally, she'd known that, but there was something about seeing evidence of his presence that really hit home.

She threw the magazine in with the others.

A drink was definitely in order if she was going to get through tonight. It wouldn't have been so bad, but her conversation with Alexis yesterday morning had left her feeling twitchy and guilty. She wasn't going to alter her plan, but she hated feeling like she was trotting all her sister's murdered dreams in front of her.

Avery pressed a hand to her stomach. It would all be worth it in the end. She just needed to stick it out long enough to get pregnant—not exactly a hardship since the sex itself was out of this world. It just would have been nice if she didn't have the sinking foreboding that her friendship with Drew might end as a result.

She shook her head. She was the worst friend ever. It didn't make sense. *She* was the one having issues as a result of the sex. From what she could tell, Drew hadn't had a problem keeping emotions out of it. And they weren't dating, so it wasn't like she'd run into a pitfall *there*.

Somehow, she didn't think she'd have had this problem if she'd gone with her original plan of in vitro fertilization.

God, she really *did* need a beer if she was going to get through babysitting tonight. She marched into her kitchen and pulled one out of her fridge. Nothing like a little alcoholic relaxation to take the edge off. She popped the cap and sighed.

Then she looked at it.

Should she really be drinking? Before she was going to watch her friends' infant daughter? While she was trying to get pregnant?

Crap. She hadn't even stopped to consider the implications. The babysitting bit alone made her a shitty person, but drinking while trying to get pregnant? Sure, plenty of people got pregnant without taking alcohol out of the equation, but should she really risk it? The thought that she might sabotage herself and end up doing all this—ruining her friendship with Drew and hurting her sister—for no reason made her eyes burn.

She poured the beer down the drain, the weight of her doubts threatening to crush her. If she'd missed that pretty huge detail, what else might she have missed? Maybe Drew was right and she was being selfish in the worst kind of way for jumping into this without spending, like, five years planning things out.

But the odds were, in five years it might be too late for her.

She set the bottle down and took a deep breath. If she was so incredibly selfish to charge ahead with this, regardless of who it hurt around her, what made her so damn sure she'd be a good mother? There was no guarantee she wouldn't trample all over her baby's emotions just like she was trampling over her sister's. Or make more stupid decisions without a thought, like she'd almost just done with Lily.

Avery sank to the floor and dropped her head to her hands. She was crazy for even trying to do this.

She was going to be the worst goddamn mother ever.

• • •

Drew knocked on the door for the second time and waited. Nothing. He glanced at his watch. He was early, but the Beast was out front and all the lights were on inside.

Maybe she was in the shower?

Hell yeah. He grinned at the thought of surprising a wet, naked Avery and opened the door. After how hot things had gotten on the side of the road yesterday, he was more than willing to follow through on his promise to get her ass into bed. It couldn't be the long, drawn-out session he'd been planning, but that was a sacrifice he was willing to make.

Then he turned through the doorway to her kitchen and froze. She was in the corner, curled into a ball on the floor, her head in her hands, her shoulders shaking.

What the fuck?

He opened his mouth to ask, but fear stilled the words before they escaped. Everything had been fine twenty-four hours ago. Hell, it'd been better than fine. What could have possibly happened in the intervening time to do *this* to her? He thought back to the last time he'd seen her this broken looking and everything went still inside him.

Holy fuck, is it the cancer?

There had been no signs in the last round of preliminary testing—not beyond her possessing the genetic markers, anyway—but she might have snuck off to the doctors without telling him. Christ. He took a deep breath and stepped into the kitchen, the creak of the squeaky floorboards under his feet giving him away.

She lifted her head and the lost look on her face ripped his heart out of his chest. "Drew?"

"I'm here, sweetheart." He crossed the remaining distance between them in a single step and went to his knees next to her. She didn't protest when he pulled her into his lap, and that told him all he needed to know about her state of mind. "Tell me what's wrong."

"Everything."

Everything did nothing to help his growing panic. He smoothed back her hair, trying to will himself to be calm. "Okay, let's take it one thing at a time."

"I can't do this."

No. He clenched his jaw against the instinctive response. "Can't do what, exactly?"

"Any of it. You. Me. Alexis. The whole thing. I'm going to be a terrible mother."

The urge to laugh at such a ridiculous statement almost made him say something stupid and make things worse. She didn't need jokes right now. She needed him to make this hurt right. The fact that he *could* make it right was a balm to his soul, because there were all too many things he was helpless to fix. "Why would you think that? You're great with Lily."

"That's because I've never been left alone with her. I'm just as likely to get drunk and let her play with knives as I am to give her a rattle."

Enough was enough. Her fears might be normal, but she was spiraling into crazy talk. "Bullshit."

She blinked at him. "What?"

"What the hell brought this on? Because you know Ryan and you know Bri, and you know as well as I do that those two would never leave someone alone with their little angel if they had doubts. Hell, they aren't even letting me babysit without *you* there, too." With good reason. He wasn't exactly Daddy Daycare material.

"But I was going to drink a beer! I didn't even stop to think that it might not be a good idea before babysitting, or that it might hurt the baby. I was only thinking about myself, just like always."

All this because of a beer? He tucked her hair behind her ears. "Is there any reason you couldn't drink?"

"You aren't supposed to drink when you're pregnant, Drew. Everyone knows that."

His heart skipped a beat. "You're pregnant?"

"What? No." She actually rolled her eyes. "It's been like thirty hours. It's way too soon to tell."

"Oh." The feelings in his chest were all tangled up, but they were mostly relief. He thought. He held her tighter, wishing he could fight away her fears as well as he fought everything else. This was one battle he felt completely inadequate for. All he knew was that Avery would be the greatest mom ever. He waited until he was sure he had her full attention. "Did your doctor think you'd have any problems having a baby?"

She shook her head. "He said he didn't see why I'd have a problem getting pregnant, as long as I did it quickly because the longer I wait, the more danger there is of the cancer showing up."

Thank God. He framed her face with his hands. "A lot of people drink and still get pregnant. One could argue that most unplanned pregnancies *start* with alcohol. I think you're good."

"I'm so scared, Drew." Her lower lip quivered. "What if I screw this up?"

"I told you before, and I'll tell you again as many times as you need to hear it—you're going to be a great mom. It's okay that you don't have things one hundred percent figured out. You'd probably be a droid if you did."

She gave a choked laugh. "I suppose that's a fair point."

"The only kind of point I make." He kissed her forehead,

driven by some impulse he couldn't name. "It'll be okay. I promise."

"You can't promise that. No one can." She sat up and scrubbed at her face. "But you're right. God, I'm sorry you had to play counselor to my crazy lady."

"You have a lot going on." And he had a feeling he wasn't helping matters much. Not that he was arrogant enough to think she was really torn up over him, but no doubt this situation they were in was just one more stressor on top of so many others.

"I told Alexis this morning."

He went still, trying to read her face. Alexis was a total darling, but Drew couldn't begin to guess how she'd reacted—not after that douche of a fiancé basically dumped her at the altar. "How'd that go?"

"She was supportive—totally and completely support-ive." She sniffed. "But I could tell that it hurt her. How could it *not* hurt her? I'm the worst sister ever."

He pulled her back against his chest and hugged her. "Sweetheart, you can't stop living your life because it might hurt your sister. Alexis has her own path to follow."

"I just feel so selfish."

"You want a baby. That's not something to be ashamed of."

She pushed against his chest until he let her lean back. "You're right. I know you're right." She sighed. "I'm freaking out over nothing, aren't I?"

Even if he'd believed that—and he wasn't sure he did because this baby-making shit was complicated—Drew never would have told her so. Not when he'd almost had a freak-out of his own when he thought she had gotten bad news regarding cancer.

She's okay. I'm not going to lose her. I refuse *to.*

"You're entitled to have your moments."

"I feel like I'm living one big moment." She shook her head. "Okay, enough. I'm sorry I blubbered all over you."

"It's fine." And, strangely enough, it was. He was serious when he'd talked to Ryan. It only stood to reason that some of those times would be while she was having a complete emotional meltdown. Hell, it would probably be worse once she actually got pregnant.

A problem for another day.

"I'm going to go…wash my face or something. Help yourself to the beer—like you always do." She disappeared down the hallway, leaving him alone with his thoughts.

Not exactly a safe place to be. The more he contemplated it, the more he didn't mind being here for Avery. It shouldn't matter. Before they had sex, would he have held her? Or would he have tried to cheer her up with their own brand of messed up humor? Laughter was the anti-crying, right?

The problem was he had no idea. He was so wrapped up in the situation that he couldn't see the light of day. No matter how hard he tried to hold on to the absolute truths he'd clung to at the beginning, the boundaries between them were changing. And he had no idea what to do about it.

Maybe it was all in his head. If so, then he'd man up and deal with it for the time being. Yeah, that sounded about right. Avery was half a step off her "normal," but that didn't mean she was experiencing things quite like he was. He could hold on until this was through. For her.

He didn't have a choice. Actually dating her wasn't an option, not when he had the legacy of Drunk Billy hanging over his head. The minute he stepped into a relationship, he became a ticking time bomb. In the past, he'd always gotten out before things got serious enough to push into the love zone, but that wasn't an option with Avery. She was his rock, the one who'd been there with him through everything. He couldn't extract himself before things got too serious because they already *were* serious. But this wasn't a relationship, and he wasn't truly going to be a father. All he had to do was see this through and keep his game face on.

Because he was her goddamn best friend and he'd do anything for her.

Chapter Ten

By the time they left her house, Avery was feeling a little bit more like herself. She still couldn't quite look Drew in the eye, but that was just fine. There would be plenty to distract her for the rest of the night so she didn't have to look too closely at her freak-out earlier.

God, what was wrong with her? Sure, she was under a lot of stress, and the thought of having to tell her grandparents what she was planning made her break out in hives, but she'd handled stress before and had never thrown her melting-down self into Drew's arms.

Pushing aside the end result, she tried to picture what her grandparents would say once she finally came clean. Dad wasn't the problem—her father just wanted her and Alexis to be happy, whatever route that took. If she showed up tomorrow and told him she was going to run off to San Francisco with her two girlfriends to form a triad, Dad would probably give her a hug, slip her some money, and tell her to call when she got there safely.

Nâinai and *Yé-ye*, though? At best, she'd get a cold, disapproving silence. At worst, she'd be in for the lecture of her life about all the ways she was a disappointment to the family, and how they were relying on *her* to continue the bloodlines their family had cultivated for generations. Most families had moved into the twenty-first century and taken a much more lax view of marriage.

Not hers.

After Alexis had her procedure, *Yé-ye* hadn't even bothered to come to the hospital to visit her. God forbid he show some support to his granddaughter who'd just gone through a traumatic surgery—not to mention the goddamn cancer—and seen her chances at having a biological child tossed out the window.

Even worse, when her sister's piece of shit fiancé took off, *Yé-ye* had told her *it served her right* for being unable to bear him children, and that no man worth his salt would stay with a woman who couldn't do the very thing women were put on this earth for.

Avery would never raise a hand to an elderly person, but she'd come dangerously close after those words came out of her grandfather's mouth.

"So, are we going to get out of the car? Or did you want to hang out in the driveway all night?"

She startled, realizing she'd been so lost in her thoughts she hadn't noticed they'd arrived. "Maybe I should go home. I'm feeling better, but what if I lose it again?" It had to be extra irresponsible to put herself in charge of an infant when she might have another meltdown.

"Nope. You're not getting out of this now. We're here.

Besides, you know damn well I can't do this alone. I need you."
When she just looked at him, he leaned over and pressed a
hand against her stomach. "And I still haven't fulfilled my
promise of getting your ass into a bed. How about an orgasm
or two later as a reward for good behavior?"

The conflicting feelings—her need to have a baby and
her desire for Drew—crashed into her, all driven by the heat
of his hand sinking through her thin T-shirt. "I—"

"Come on. We're late." He turned off the engine and got
out of the car.

She half expected him to bound up to the covered porch
and leave her sitting there, but he turned around and stuck
his hands in his pockets, obviously intending to wait.

Or tackle her if she tried to take off.

She could do this. A night of babysitting wasn't the end
of the world. And, really, the only other option she had was
sitting at home, driving herself crazy with her worries over
the future.

So she slipped out of the truck and met him at the front
of the hood. Drew surprised her by framing her face with his
big hands. "I'm going to be in hell all night thinking about
getting you naked."

Whoa. So much had changed in such a short time. A few
days ago she and Drew had been firmly and happily in the
friend zone, and now he was spending time thinking about
getting her naked? If she wasn't careful, she'd get caught
up in the sizzling chemistry and forget that this had an end
game—and an expiration date. Once she was pregnant, there
would be no nookie. They'd go back to being friends—and
only friends.

It seemed like he was forgetting that important little

fact, but hopefully he was just better at compartmentalizing than she was. She cleared her throat. "Oh yeah?"

"Yeah. Knowing what's inside those tiny shorts makes me crazy. I want to haul you into my truck cab and yank them off. Do you know how long it's been since I tasted you?" He leaned in, his presence stealing her words more effectively than if he'd kissed them away. "*Ages*, Avery."

Okaaaay. Definitely compartmentalizing. Her body threatened to melt into a puddle at his feet, but she straightened her spine, and tried to keep the breathiness from her voice. If he could compartmentalize, she could, too. To prove it to herself, she took his hand and pressed it to the V between her legs. "Guess you'd better get to it, then, huh?"

"Jesus."

The sound of the front door opening had them jumping apart. Thank God Bri had a screened-in porch or Ryan would have seen exactly how close his brother and Avery were to getting busy in the driveway.

"Are you guys coming in or what?"

"Yep!" She started for the porch door, giving Drew a little finger wave. The look on his face let her know she was going to pay for that something fierce later on.

Good. Now she really had something to look forward to tonight.

• • •

The babysitting gig started off easily enough, mostly because Lily was napping when Bri handed them a list of things they needed to know and kept biting her lip until Ryan physically hustled her out of the house. It was strangely cute seeing how protective she was. She'd come a long way from the shy woman who'd moved to Wellingford a little over two years ago.

The door shut behind them and Drew dropped onto the couch. "Come here."

Avery laughed from her place on the other side of the coffee table. "Thanks, but I've heard this one before."

"This may be hard to believe, but I'm not going to throw you down on this couch and ravish you in my brother's house." Though he wasn't about to lie and say it didn't hold a certain amount of appeal. He pointed at the TV. "*Jeopardy* is on."

"We haven't done this in awhile." She dropped onto the cushion next to him, not quite close enough to touch, but also not on the other side, like she would have normally done.

It was…nice.

They hummed the theme music and then looked at each other and laughed. Drew waggled his eyebrows at her, glad to have her happy again. "Is Alex Trebeck on your list?"

She made a face. "Don't be gross. He has all the markings of a dirty birdy."

He started to respond—what the hell made this older guy gross and the others she ooohed over hot?—but froze when a wail cut through the air. "What the hell is that?"

"That, genius, is your niece." She stood, took a deep breath, and disappeared down the hallway to where the baby's room had been set up. Drew was still trying to decide if he should follow and offer to help—though, seriously, what was he going to bring to the table?—when she reappeared with Lily in her arms. "Here, hold her while I heat up a bottle."

Then she just passed over the baby and walked away.

Every muscle in his body tensed up holding the tiny wailing bundle. He hadn't held Lily much since she was born three months ago, though he'd been around quite a bit. It was just absolutely terrifying to be even partially responsible for her well-being.

Hell, what if he dropped her? Or held her too tightly?

"Just relax, Drew." Avery's voice drifted in from the kitchen. "The baby isn't going to shatter in a million pieces if you get comfortable."

Of course she knew how uncomfortable he was with this. She knew he liked kids, but babies weren't the same thing as kids. They were little balls of fury and hunger. Bracing himself, he scooted deeper into the couch, until his back rested against it. Now, at least, he wasn't in danger of muscle spasms. He looked down at his niece, marveling at how much she'd changed in three short months. When he first saw her, she looked like an angry old man, all wrinkly and red. Now, she actually looked like a tiny person.

Though she was still red as all get-out from the crying.

Without meaning to, he rocked a little, dipping back and forth. Almost immediately, her cries quieted and she made a gurgling sound that was shockingly cute. "There, now. That's not so bad." His heart melted a little at her cute coo as he rocked her. He could get used to this tiny weight in his hands. Hell, he'd *better* get used to it, because if his and Avery's plan was successful, there'd be another baby showing up all too soon.

He studied Lily's features, from her impossibly blue eyes to the dark tuft of hair on her nearly bald head. What would his baby look like? Would it be a cute little girl like Lily? Or maybe a husky boy? It didn't matter. Whatever baby came from Avery would be fucking perfect.

Drew smiled. "Who's a pretty baby?" He laughed when she cooed again. What had he been so freaked out about? This wasn't so bad. It struck him that a few minutes had passed without anything traumatic happening, and Avery wasn't even in the room making sure he didn't mess up.

There was something so peaceful about sitting here, holding a baby in his arms, while he listened to Avery putter around the kitchen. It was…domestic, something he'd never once allowed himself to picture—a future with a family.

Lily looked at him and, for one long moment, he thought they had an understanding. Then she squinted up her eyes and let loose a wail loud enough to wake the dead.

He jumped, and tried to stop the motion halfway through, which sent a painful spasm through his entire body. "*Avery*."

"I'm here. It's okay." She swept in with a bottle in one hand and a dishtowel in the other. "Here."

He took the bottle and stared at it. "Thanks?"

"Give it to Lily." Her hands guided his, helping him ease the bottle's nipple into the baby's mouth. Instantly, all crying ceased as Lily set to the milk with an intensity that gave him the heebie-jeebies. A minute passed. And then another. All without another screaming jag. If anything, Lily looked blissed out, her eyes sliding partially shut.

He grinned at Avery. "I'm doing it."

"Yes, you are. See, it's not so bad." She used the towel to wipe a dribble off the baby's cheek. Her smile lit up the room.

They could do this. They could actually do the thing he'd never let himself consider before—do the family thing successfully. Drew stroked his thumb over Lily's cheek, feeling like his chest would burst with all the feelings bubbling up inside him. It could be *his* baby in his arms.

It was scary how much he wanted that.

• • •

Avery had Lily in bed, well fed and with a clean diaper, by the time Ryan and Bri made it back from their date. Her best friend was the first one through the door and she looked a bit flushed. She gave them both a bright smile. "How'd everything go?"

Drew laughed. "Terribly. Can't you smell the smoke?" He didn't even flinch when Avery smacked him.

"You know damn well I'm the only one in the family who gets to make fire jokes." Ryan came through the door and nearly bowled Bri over before he caught himself. It was hard to tell in this light, but she thought she detected the beginnings of a hickey low on his neck. Apparently they'd put their date night to good use.

"I don't know. My niece might have the firebug gene."

Ryan shook his head. "You'd better hope not, or you're going to be the one scaring the shit out of her, Uncle Sheriff."

"I'm going to do that anyways." Drew frowned. "And any idiot boy who looks at her sideways."

Ryan laughed. "Do you have time for a beer before you two take off?"

"Sure."

The men headed into the kitchen and Bri dropped onto

the couch by Avery's feet. She moved them so her friend had more space. "Have fun?"

"What?"

Avery sat up. "With your little roadside nookie. Did you have fun? Take out any road signs? Set anything on fire?" She grinned. The last time Ryan and Bri had decided to make out while driving, they'd nearly taken out half of Main Street.

"God, when are you going to let that go? It was one tiny traffic light, and a small blue mailbox. Over a *year* ago."

"You and Ryan took out the only traffic light in Wellingford. I'm pretty sure I have at least five more years of jokes left before I have to move on."

"Typical." Then a grin broke over Bri's face. "But yes, I did have fun."

I bet. It was all too easy for Avery to jump into the memory of her own roadside session yesterday...and start thinking about what tonight's happy ending might look like.

No. No thinking about sex with Drew in front of Bri.

"Look at you," Avery teased to redirect her train of thought, "sneaking off after a fancy date to have a quickie with your husband. It's like I don't even know you anymore."

Bri blushed. "New babies change everything. I'm just *finally* starting to have enough energy to...do things. And I was so nervous about leaving Lily alone—even with you two—that Ryan decided I needed a distraction. Twice."

Go, Ryan. Everyone seemed to be getting busy these days. "Hey, you don't have to justify it to me. I'm totally thrilled to babysit anytime you guys want to destroy more public property in your quest for orgasms."

"Shush. They'll hear you." Bri looked like she was going

to say something else, but then the Flannery brothers came back into the room.

Drew smiled at Avery. "You ready to get out of here?" *And into bed*, his eyes said.

Holy hell, yes. He didn't have to ask her twice. Which was worrisome in a big way, because sex with Drew was only a means to an end. It had to be. She almost tripped over Bri when she jumped off the couch. "Yeah, it's getting late. And I'm sure you two would like some more alone time."

Bri muttered something, but then Drew took Avery's hand and that was all she could focus on. She paused at the door and glanced back. "Let me know if you guys need another date night."

"You might have to arm wrestle Marcy for the privilege. She called dibs on the next one."

Bri's next door neighbor, Marcy, was one of their tiny town's elementary school teachers, so it went without saying that she was great with kids. Her own daughter was only four, but precocious as all get-out, and if Marcy's new husband — one of Drew's deputies, as fate would have it — had anything to say about it, they'd be adding to the family soon.

Everyone seemed to be having babies these days. Avery pressed a hand against her stomach. *I hope to God I'm one of them soon.* She managed a smile. "Fine, but I get the one after that." Everything had gone swimmingly tonight. And watching Drew feed his niece would have been enough to jumpstart her ovaries if she wasn't already trying to get pregnant. The way he'd grinned when he realized he was doing it on his own… God, her entire body had lit up in response.

How could she want him this much? Okay, that was a stupid question. Like it or not, they had a few decades' worth of pent-up sexual frustration, and the real-life sex was the best she'd ever had. So, of course she was going to want him all the damn time. But her earlier meltdown was behind her. They could keep this in its neat little box. It would hurt to let it go, but she was strong enough to survive that.

She hoped.

Chapter Eleven

They'd barely made it out the door before Drew's phone rang. He cursed—because no one called him at ten on a weeknight to just say hello—and answered. "Flannery."

"We've, ah, got a situation." His deputy, Aaron, didn't sound any happier to be calling than Drew was to take the call. "Group of kids—seniors—thought it'd be a good idea to go streaking down Main Street."

Shit. "And tonight the bridge club is playing down at the coffee shop." Which no doubt had given them a front-row seat.

Aaron sighed. "Miss Nora Lee called to report it. She's not happy."

No, she wouldn't be. She had a high tolerance for she-nanigans and pranks, but nudity wasn't acceptable in her worldview. No doubt she was livid. "You have the kids in custody?"

"Yeah, all six of them are in our free cell. I've started

calling the parents, but—"

"They're going to want to talk to me." Thank God he'd only had two beers tonight, or this would be even more of a nightmare. Then Drew registered what Aaron had said. "Why is there only one cell open?"

He hesitated. "Rusty is in the other. He got pushy with Gena during the evening shift, and then tried to swing on me when I went to go pick him up. I figured it'd be safer for everyone if I let him sleep it off here."

Fuck. The last thing he wanted was to deal with Rusty tonight, on top of what was going to be a headache's worth of furious parents. "I'll be there as soon as I can. Ten, fifteen minutes, tops."

"Roger that."

He hung up and turned to Avery, but she was already smiling. "Duty calls?"

"Apparently a group of our graduating seniors thought it would be a good idea to go streaking down Main Street."

She laughed. "Sounds like us when we were that age."

"If I remember correctly—and I do—you couldn't be persuaded to take off your underwear. So, technically, we weren't streaking."

"A lady has to have standards." She grinned. "If you need to get going ASAP, I can just get a ride home from Ryan. I'm sure he hasn't dragged Bri to the bedroom quite yet."

"Speaking of dragging someone to bed—" He stepped into her space and gripped her hips, pulling her against him. "I'll be by later."

"Oh, really?"

"Yeah." He thrust against her, loving how her eyes went

hazy. "You were good tonight. That's got to be rewarded."

She smiled, slow and sweet. "Sounds like a plan to me. Now go put the fear of God into those teenagers." Avery turned and sauntered up the steps to the porch, pausing just outside the screen door to send him a scorching look.

Fuck. Drew shook his head, adjusted his pants, and climbed into his truck. The sooner he got there, the sooner he could get back to her place and inside her.

The station was a madhouse, and two sets of parents were yelling at each other as he walked through the door. They froze when they caught sight of him, and he knew he was in for it. He held up a hand. "Give me a minute to get things sorted out, and we'll get your kids released."

"Released?" A woman stepped forward, and his chest sank when he recognized Dannie Lane, the pastor's wife. "There has to be some mistake. My Jessie wouldn't be caught dead doing something like *this*, let alone with that troublemaker John Hart."

Considering the rumors he'd heard about Dannie's own experimentation in college, he didn't think she had a leg to stand on with those kinds of accusations. Not that Drew would say as much—his job was to calm things down, not rile everyone up.

"Hey!" And that would be John Hart's parents. His dad crossed his arms over his chest. "My son is a good boy. It's *your* girl who keeps getting him into trouble."

As he stepped between both sets of parents, he resigned himself to this being one hell of a long night.

• • •

By the time Drew made it to Avery's place, he was dead on his feet. The drama hadn't lessened as more parents arrived, each determined to blame someone else for the actions of their teenager. All he'd had to do was take a look at the guilty expression on the six kids' faces to know that no one made any of them do a damn thing.

And all the while, Rusty had been pacing his cell, running into the bars and the wall with every other step, barely able to keep himself on his feet. That hadn't stopped him from ranting about his bitch ex-wife. Drew almost felt sorry for the kids being forced to listen to that bullshit. He sure as hell could have gone without.

He'd half considered just going home and sleeping the whole thing off, but he craved the feeling of Avery in his arms. It was selfish, but he didn't care. He pounded on her door, half surprised when she opened it a few seconds later, and leaned against the frame, blinking at him. Dressed in a pair of gray sweatpants with their high school logo on them, and a white tank top, she was everything he needed.

"I thought you might have changed your mind."

The nonchalant way she talked about him no-call-no-showing set his teeth on edge. "Things were a little more complicated than I expected. I'm an asshole for taking forever. Forgive me?"

"When duty calls, duty calls." She stepped back. "Come on in."

He followed her down the hall to the living room where she must have passed out on the couch, judging from the blanket and television turned down so low he could barely make out the words. She yawned as she folded the blanket and tossed it into the coffee table chest in the middle of the room. "I'm on the far side of exhausted, so maybe we could make this a quick one?"

Now that he was at her place, all he really wanted was to sit down, pull her into his lap, and just *be*. But she was standing there, patiently waiting for him to follow her to the bedroom so they could just get it over with. Drew forced himself to keep the tension out of his voice. "You mind if I use your shower?" He needed a few minutes to wash away the last few hours and get his head on straight.

"By all means. I'll meet you in the bedroom." She disappeared around the corner, leaving him staring after her.

Cursing himself for making things more complicated than they needed to be, he headed for the bathroom down the hall. This should be easy. He was here to make a baby, not rock her world in bed, or to seek comfort after a shitty evening. He wasn't built for anything beyond superficial stuff like sex and both he and Avery knew it. But his needs were all conflicted and twisted up inside him. Nothing seemed simple anymore. Everything that had previously been black and white now held only shades of gray.

The shower took longer than his normal five minute scrub-down because he was still arguing with himself over whether he should talk to Avery about the change in their dynamic, or wait and hope things went back to normal after she got pregnant.

He turned off the water before he made a decision, and dried off quickly. He had a spare set of clothes that he kept there, but they were in her room, so he wrapped the towel around his waist and walked out of the bathroom.

She was sound asleep, curled into a ball in the middle of her bed. "Avery?" When she didn't so much as stir, he moved to the dresser drawer she kept for him on the nights he needed to crash on her couch for one reason or another, and pulled on a pair of sweats.

He felt too guilty to wake her a second time—especially since he wasn't sure what the hell he wanted anymore. He probably should have just gone home, but he didn't want to leave. Was he running the risk of complicating things beyond repair? Hell yes. But he was too far gone to care.

Drew crawled onto the bed. He smoothed back her hair, and smiled when she didn't even shift. He'd seen Avery jump out of a dead sleep with fists flying when someone messed with her while she was sleeping, but she didn't flinch from his touch. She trusted him. It was something he'd known— he trusted her with his life, too—but this felt different than what they'd had before. This was deeper, more profound, just *more*.

He shifted closer, until his chest pressed against her back and he wrapped an arm around her waist. He pressed a kiss to her neck, closed his eyes, and finally let the bullshit from the day drift away.

· · ·

Avery gradually became aware of the body at her back, one heavy arm draped over her stomach. She had a moment of confusion because there was a man there, and there shouldn't be, but it died before it could take root, as her body instinctively recognized him. *Drew*. Drew was sleeping in her bed, his breath ruffling the back of her neck.

What the hell happened? The last thing she remembered was dropping onto her bed in resignation, and exhaustion finally pulling her eyelids closed.

Apparently Drew had decided to stay instead of waking her up. This wasn't part of the deal, but she couldn't bring herself to mind. It felt too good to be wrapped up in him.

This was what Ryan and Bri had every night. It was this, even more than the sex, which she craved. And now Drew was giving it to her.

She glanced at the bedside clock, wincing when its red numbers showed 3 a.m. Too early or too late, depending on how she looked at it. She rolled over, marveling at how different he looked when he slept. What a cliché. Of course he looked different. For one, he was perfectly still, aside from the faint rise and fall of his chest as he breathed. Usually when Drew walked into a room, everyone knew it, even if he didn't say anything. He just had that kind of energy. Now, he looked like a normal guy, if a ruggedly gorgeous one, with his faint beard and slightly too-long dark hair.

Before she could talk herself out of it, she reached up and smoothed back a wave that stood out from the rest. From there it seemed the most natural thing in the world to slide her hand down the side of his face to his jaw. His stubble rasped against her palm, and he murmured something too softly for her to make out.

What would it be like to wake up to him every morning?

It was something she'd never really let herself consider, because putting too much thought into an impossible future was a great way to end up in a nuthouse. But it didn't feel impossible right now, with his body warm against her and his low breathing sounding through the bedroom. No matter how much she tried to keep everything separate in her mind over the last few days, things had definitely shifted between them. It was more than the sex, though that was a game changer no matter which way she looked at it. The goal of a baby had shifted her perspective, had her looking more toward the future, and she couldn't help wondering if that future would have moments like this with Drew—soft and sweet enough to wrap around her heart and never let go. It was just so *right* having him there. She loved it.

And she was in some serious trouble.

But worrying about it wasn't going to do anything but stress her out. She might as well roll with it, for better or worse.

Emboldened by the thought, she shifted closer and pressed an openmouthed kiss against his neck. He moved, lacing his fingers through her hair, but didn't seem to actually wake up.

It signified something she wasn't sure she was ready to follow through with, so she focused on the fact that it gave her free rein to enjoy him in a way she'd never been allowed before. In their sexual encounters up to this point, he'd taken full control and she'd just been swept along on the orgasm roller coaster. Not that she was complaining, but she wanted to actually *touch* him before this thing between them reached its expiration date.

She ran her fingers over his chest, enjoying his well-defined pecs. Drew was in killer shape, and his upper body could seriously fill out a T-shirt. She leaned down and flicked his nipple with her tongue, before moving further south.

His breathing changed as she hovered over the waistband

of his sweats, saving her from the debate of if she was really going to make a move on him while he was sleeping. "You going to stop there?"

She looked up to find his eyes open. Stop? Not a chance. "I'm considering."

"Keep it up and I might have to jump you instead."

No way was she missing this chance. "Shh. It's my turn to drive things tonight.

She hooked his waistband and pulled it down over his hips, the sight of his cock temporarily stealing her breath. She'd seen him naked a few times, but the impact only seemed to be growing instead of decreasing like it should. *Nothing* about this was going like it should, from the sex to the forbidden emotions welling up in her chest. She didn't want to think about that, though. Not now, maybe not ever.

The only thing she *did* want occupying her headspace was how good it felt to touch him. She slid down a little further to get comfortable and then gave his cock a slow stroke. Truth be told, she could play with him all night, but she didn't think his patience would hold for that kind of treatment unless he was tied down.

An idea for later maybe…

She licked up the underside of his cock, earning a hissed breath. Emboldened, she took him in her mouth, as deep as she could manage, mirroring the slow stroke she'd just done with her hand. Drew cursed, his hands spasming in her hair. Power beat through her. She could drive him out of his mind like this, with just her mouth and her hands. It would be the easiest thing in the world. She moved to shallower strokes, using her tongue to swirl around the head of his cock.

"Avery, I—" She met his gaze as she licked him, and

Drew cursed again, louder. "Holy fuck. Come here."

He didn't give her much of a chance to argue as he pulled her up his body, and she kicked off her sweatpants. Since she wasn't wearing any underwear, it was easy work from there to straddle his hips. He ran his hands up her sides. "I'd say turnabout is fair play, but I'm going to lose it if I taste you right now."

The rough comment only served to stoke her need for him higher. Most of her exes could take oral or leave it, and even the ones who claimed to enjoy giving it didn't come close to the need she heard in Drew's voice when he said things like that.

God, she was going to miss that.

She focused on his hard length sliding against her. She needed him inside her and she needed it now. "You know, you're setting a pretty damn high bar for my future husband to live up to. He's going to have to be a rock star in the sack to even come close to this."

He paused, his whole body going tense beneath her. For half a second, she worried that she'd pissed him off, but then he said, "Better prepare yourself—that bar is going to be higher after tonight." He held her hips, rocking her against him but keeping them pressed together too tightly for her to change the angle. "You're wet, sweetheart. I think you like giving as much as I do."

"Maybe." She gasped when he slid against her clit.

"Maybe? Now you're just being mean."

How the hell could he call her mean when he was teasing like this? "What are you going to do about it?" Bang her into submission, hopefully.

He grinned, a flash of teeth in the shadows. "I have a

few ideas." He lifted her and tilted his hips, and then he was inside her.

Avery let her eyes drift close as she moved on him, trying not to acknowledge how addicting it was having Drew inside her. It was a lost cause. *She* was a lost cause. "I think I like your brand of punishment." *I like it too much to be good for me.*

"Thought you might." He urged her on as she rolled her hips, grinding against him. "Just like that, sweetheart. Show me how you like it."

She liked everything he did to her—in and out of the bedroom—and that truth lodged in her throat. In the here and now, Avery gave herself over to the feeling of him stretching her, pressing against all the right places. All too soon, the indecipherable feeling started winding through her. It remained just out of reach, teasing her.

"Tell me what you need."

Everything. Luckily, she bit her lips before the word could slip free. "Touch me."

Immediately he moved one hand, pressing against her clit in counterpoint with each stroke. Her pleasure spiked, stars exploding behind her eyelids. Drew's fingers dug into her hips and he pounded into her, sending her over the edge as he groaned and came. "Fuck."

She collapsed onto his chest, trying not to read into it when he started tracing abstract patterns over her back. She closed her eyes and just luxuriated in the afterglow, her body feeling deliciously used. She could get used to this. To *all* of this.

Time passed, the minutes stretching out until the afterglow faded and reality started to set back in. She stopped touching him, but he kept her against his chest with a hand on her back. It struck her that he'd stayed and voluntarily climbed into her bed with the goal of sleeping and not banging like bunnies.

This wasn't part of the deal. What am I supposed to say now?

Her awkwardness grew alongside the tension in her body. She had to say something to break this silence, but everything she came up with would only make things *more* awkward.

"I'm starving."

Trust Drew to focus on the basics and ignore the potential emotional downfalls. She really could learn a thing or two from him on compartmentalizing. Avery laughed and rolled off him. "Way to ruin the moment."

"We had a moment. Now it's over and I'm hungry."

"You're always thinking with your stomach." She stood and tossed a pillow at his face.

"You say that like it's a bad thing." He headed out of the bedroom and, a few seconds later, she heard the bathroom door shut. She took the opportunity to grab a pair of panties and her discarded sweats.

She made it to the kitchen the same time he did, and it was everything she could do not to stare at his bare chest. Despite having seen him shirtless more times than she could count, it felt different now that she'd had her mouth all over that skin. She wanted to do it again.

"What do you have in the way of sandwich makings?"

Right. Food. She opened the fridge. "The usual. PB&J, turkey, ham."

"Let's throw together some turkey and ham."

She grabbed both meats and the sliced cheese. "You're disgusting."

"Hey now, I can't help that I have distinguished tastes while yours are totally lacking."

"Says the man who likes hot sauce on every single food group."

Drew grinned and started piling the meat on his bread. "You haven't lived until you've tried hot sauce on Granny Smith apples."

"Thanks, but I'll pass." But she was smiling as she wrapped a slice of turkey around her cheese and bit down. It was hard to get too into the spirit of bickering—or worried about the future—when she was still glowing from that orgasm. No wonder so many people said sex was the foundation of a relationship—it would be impossible to have terrible fights when she spent most of her day walking around feeling like this.

Yeah, time to dial that back in.

They ate in silence, and Drew demolished his two sandwiches in record time and then started fidgeting. "So… I was thinking…"

If he took off right now, it would be a blow, no matter if that was the original agreement or not. It wasn't fair that she felt that way—not to him or to her—so she pasted a smile on her face and waited for him to stop circling and spit it out. "Yeah?"

He wouldn't quite meet her eyes. "It's late."

She fought against the insane desire to feed him the excuses he'd need to leave. Or stay. Hell, she wasn't sure *what* she wanted anymore. "Sure is."

"What I'm trying to say is that I'm fucking exhausted."

He shook his head. "Damn it, that's just an excuse. The truth is, I want to stay."

She found herself holding her breath. "You want to stay."

"If you want me to. I know this wasn't part of the plan, but—" He cursed and ran a hand through his hair. "Forget it. I'm out of line."

Avery practically threw herself at him. She grabbed his face and tipped it down so he couldn't avoid looking at her. "I'd like you to stay."

"All night?"

"Drew, it's like four in the morning, but yes—all night."

His slow smile did a number on her mental health. "Then let's go to bed."

If she had any question about his planning to jump her again, it was laid to rest as he crawled onto the bed behind her and pulled the covers up around them. He tucked in against her back, and smoothed her hair up and over the pillow before placing a kiss on the back of her neck. Her entire body tingled at the feeling of his lips there, and a sinking sensation in her chest told Avery her response had nothing to do with sexual attraction.

Shit, shit, shit.

Chapter Twelve

Avery stared into the empty coffee bag and fought back the ridiculous urge to cry. When she'd woken up this morning alone, all she'd wanted was some of the good stuff to chase away the strange twisting in her stomach. Because Drew was gone, and she had no right to be surprised. He was *always* gone after encounters like this. Hadn't he joked about being the Gotta-Go-Guy after hookups?

Why was there no coffee?

Oh yeah, because Drew had forgotten to bring her another bag like he'd promised. She sighed and threw the empty bag away. It wasn't a big deal. He forgot stuff all the time. It wasn't some kind of sign from the universe that she was about to be kicked in the teeth. All she had to do was stop by the coffee shop on her way to work. Easy.

But even a long shower and her favorite T-shirt—a Browncoat one Drew had bought her a few years ago—weren't enough to shake the mood threatening. She stepped out of her house and took a deep breath, trying to enjoy the fresh air, but the cloud cover overhead wasn't exactly inspiring.

The walk helped—getting moving and stretching her legs usually quieted the worries circling her head—and she reached the coffee shop all too soon. Avery waved at Old Joe as she placed her order. "Hey, Joe."

"Good morning, Miss Avery." He lifted a cup full of what would be green tea. As far as she knew, Joe didn't touch coffee, which was a crying shame. "We don't usually see you around here so early."

"I ran out of my stuff." She tipped the barista and took her paper cup, the warmth that soaked into her hands instantly making her feel better. "How're you?"

"Oh, you know me. Just plugging along." His eyes twinkled. "My grandson is visiting next week, you know."

She laughed. "Joe, your grandson is twenty-two years old. He's practically a baby."

"And what better way to keep you young and fresh but a younger man? He thinks the world of you."

Because she'd been guilted into letting him take her out for a drink last time he came around. Warren was a nice guy but he was just too…not Drew. She pressed her lips together, wishing she could banish that thought. It was no use. It was the goddamn truth. This week had only cemented that. If no guy measured up to him before, they sure as hell wouldn't be able to now. Damn it.

"Unless you have a certain someone already?"

She blinked, belatedly realizing she'd been lost in thought. "What? Everyone knows I'm not dating anyone."

"You and the older Flannery boy are attached at the

hip, though. Have been since you were yay tall." He held his hand up to indicate just how young they were.

"It's not like that with Drew." It tasted like a lie, because it *was* becoming like that with him. She had to get out of there before Old Joe ferretted that particular piece of information out of her. If he did, it'd spread like wildfire through Wellingford that poor Avery Yeung was holding a torch for playboy Drew Flannery, and that was the last thing she wanted. She patted Joe's hand. "It was nice seeing you, but I've got to run or I'll be opening my shop late."

"Have a good day, Miss Avery."

She hustled outside and down the street, fishing her keys out of her pocket as she walked. There were people out on the street, and it was enough of an effort to put a smile on her face and wave to them as she passed—she didn't think she could handle any more actual conversations.

Her shop was thankfully silent. She closed the door behind her and leaned against it. It would be okay. Here, surrounded by so much history, it would be okay. She did a circuit of the room, pausing to touch her favorite pieces.

The heavy green armoire she'd found on a trip to Pittsburgh, hidden away in the back of a thrift shop. She hadn't had the heart to sell it yet, but eventually its time would come. The jewelry tree filled with a handful of silver necklaces, each old enough that the silver was in desperate need of oxidation. That was for whoever bought it to decide, though. She loved the weight of years each one seemed to contain, loved to picture the women who must have worn them when they were shiny and new. And, finally, to her newest piece. The baby buggy.

She'd stumbled over it a month or so ago in Philadelphia,

and it had seemed like a sign that she should put her fears aside and grab life by the horns.

Her phone rang as she turned on the *Open* sign and headed for the back room. Since it was her cell and not the shop phone, she figured it must be Drew. Who else would be calling her this early? "What?"

A long silence greeted her. "Good morning, Avery."

Shit. It was her grandfather. She forced a smile into her voice even though she felt like "accidentally" hanging up. "What can I do for you, *Yé-ye*?"

"We haven't seen you in several weeks. Your grandmother is getting worried."

God forbid she do something as terrible as make *Nâinai* worry. "Tell her I'm sorry. I've been very busy with work." And Drew. And, hell, she didn't make a habit of seeking out her grandparents any more than she had to.

"While we understand the importance of work, your family should be your first priority."

How her grandfather could convey an entire lecture into a single sentence was a mystery to her. She sighed. "Yes, I know. And of course my family is my first priority."

"Even Alexis comes out for dinner at least once a week."

And, God knew, even considering that, she was still a great disappointment to them. They made sure to tell her, at least once, every time they were in the same room as her. Avery didn't get why Alexis kept coming around for more emotional abuse, but *she* wasn't that much of a masochist. "I just had lunch with Dad last Friday."

"Your father." *Yé-ye* sniffed. And that was that. He didn't need to say any more. Even though she was pretty sure her grandparents loved their only son, he had a permanent black mark on his record because he'd met an American in school, fallen in love, and had the audacity to marry her and then procreate. Avery hadn't even met her grandparents until after Mom died—without her presence in the house, they decided they could finally forgive their son. She was sure there was more to it, but at the time it'd seemed like they showed up one day and never left.

Her grandfather kept talking. "Alexis is coming for dinner on Monday night. You will be there as well."

It was always like this with *Yé-ye*. Everything was a command, as if they were all little marionettes that only came alive when he had use for them. He didn't care if she already had plans, or if she was working. He had decreed they would have a family dinner on Monday and so it would be.

Which effectively took away any excuse she had for holding off telling her family about her decision. They were going to freak out no matter when she told them. She might as well do it now and get it over with. "I'll be there."

"Goodbye, Avery."

"Goodbye, *Yé-ye*."

She hung up and dropped the phone on the counter. Family. Endlessly complicated. She would have given a lot to avoid the dinner, but it was time to face the music—or the firing squad, depending on how she wanted to look at it. She reached for her phone, and then paused, not sure what she planned. No, that wasn't right. She knew exactly what she wanted to do. She wanted to call Drew, to hear his voice and wrap the memory of him telling her that she'd be a good mother around her like a cloak. It might not be enough to protect her from the upcoming dinner, but it'd be a comfort she desperately needed.

Maybe she'd give it a little longer. She could call him around lunchtime and it wouldn't seem like she was clinging after what happened last night. Or, rather, what *didn't* happen.

Who knew *not* having sex would screw with her mind more effectively than the sex had?

. . .

Drew slouched on his couch, absently running his hand down the seam of the cushion next to him to where it was almost worn through. It was Avery's spot on the nights they ended up at his place to play games. Normally, he barely registered it, but now it seemed all too apparent. She wasn't there. Hell, that was the whole point of sneaking off this morning like some kind of thief, so he didn't have to face her—didn't have to face the reality of how much things had changed between them. Her laughing comment last night was evidence enough of that.

Despite everything, she still planned on moving on and marrying someone else.

He shouldn't be so damn surprised by that—it wasn't like someone as amazing as Avery was going to be single forever. And Drew was the guy whose longest relationship was less than six months. Rationally, it made sense that he'd never factored into the equation. In the back of his mind, he'd always known she would settle down with someone else.

But it was different now.

Now he'd gotten a taste of what a life like that could be like. A life with a woman like her and a baby in his arms. A life of coming home to a warm bed. A life with a *home*.

And she was taking it away before he had a chance to really get used to the idea. It didn't matter what he did—he'd never be able to fuck the idea of that future husband who wasn't him out of her. She might joke about being ruined, but *he* was the one who wasn't going to survive this.

With a sigh, he forced his hand away from the cushion. Sitting here, brooding the day away, wasn't going to change anything. He needed to do something, *anything* to get his mind off Avery.

To stop obsessing about the fact that *he was going to lose her*.

His gaze drifted over the blank TV. He'd bought a handful of movies last week, but he couldn't bring himself to get off the couch and put them in. Because the truth was, he'd bought them with Avery in mind. She loved corny action flicks as much as he did, and her commentary was usually his favorite part of watching.

Sure, he could work through some more of the latest *Assassin's Creed*, but the thought held no appeal. *Nothing* did. Goddamn it.

He pushed to his feet and paced around the coffee table, stopping at the mantle filled with pictures. Avery was in nearly every one. He picked up the frame with the one from the trip they'd taken to NYC a few years back, both of them grinning and wearing shirts that read *I only like NY as a friend*. Then there was the one with her and Alexis and Ryan, when they'd gone camping after Ryan graduated high school. They all held s'mores, and Avery's was burnt to a crisp. He'd given her tons of shit over the one thing she somehow managed not to be able to cook.

Drew stopped at the end of the mantle, his smile dying. The old picture was tucked behind a few more recent frames, where it was easy to forget, but he'd never been able to bring himself to throw it away. It was one of the last ones taken of their family before everything fell apart. His mother looked fresh and young and filled with joy, and even Billy managed a smile, though it was aimed at his wife. Drew was in front of them, looking so small at four, with his arm thrown around a two-year-old Ryan's shoulders. They were happy, totally unaware that it was all going to go down the shitter less than a year in the future. That they'd lose his mother, the glue that held their family together. That Billy would try to hold it together—would even succeed for a few years—but would eventually give in to the siren call of alcohol, to dull the pain he never seemed able to escape.

And then everything would fall to Drew. God, he was barely seven when he first started doing laundry so that he and Ryan had clean clothes to wear. He'd had to steal money out of Billy's wallet and sweet-talk Miss Nora Lee to go with him to buy new clothes when Ryan hit a growth spurt and suddenly nothing fit.

Seven.

And it only got worse from there.

He tucked the picture back into its spot and turned away, hating the dark turn his thoughts had taken. It was a long time ago, but he never quite shook those memories. Avery had been the one bright spot of his childhood—and later. She always seemed to know when things started weighing too heavily on him, because she'd come up with some mad scheme that he was only too happy to go along with. When her mother passed, he returned the favor. Those little adventures saved them both from the uglier emotions that always seemed ready to take over.

But thoughts of her weren't any brighter today. It was too easy to remember the feel of Lily in his arms and imagine a different baby there. *His* baby.

If she married someone else, that man would be the one raising his kid.

He was so lost in thought, he almost missed the sound of his phone ringing. It blared through the living room, and for a long moment he actually debated not answering. With his luck, it was Dannie Lane again, demanding he get her precious daughter out of the community service he'd sentenced all the kids to.

The name on the caller ID nearly had him setting the phone down again. Avery. But he couldn't do that, no matter how screwed up he felt right now. "Flannery."

"Are you busy?"

Busy? Sure. He had a full schedule of wandering his house for the next eight hours, brooding about things he wasn't sure he could change. "I can spare a few minutes."

"I hadn't heard from you, so I thought I'd just check in and see what the plan was for tonight?" The phone rustled, as if she was pacing the same way he currently was. "Maybe we could grab dinner before we got down to business?"

He wanted to. Christ, how he wanted to. But Drew was already shaking his head, a lie springing to life. "Can't. I'm pulling a double today." Even if it wasn't an out-and-out lie, it was a flimsy excuse. Doubles were exhausting, but they'd never kept him from seeing Avery before.

"Oh."

She sounded so disappointed, he wanted to reach

through the phone and hug her, but Drew wasn't going to be good company for anyone today. Add in his confusion from everything going on with Avery, and he needed space to think and get his head on straight. "It'll have to wait until tomorrow."

"Yeah, sure. See you then. Later." She hung up, leaving him once again alone with his thoughts.

It was a shitty ass place to be.

Chapter Thirteen

By the time she closed her shop, Avery had a plan to let off some steam. After getting her sister to agree, she dialed Bri.

"Hi, Avery."

"Hi." She moved a few things around on the new table she'd bought and tried to decide if she liked the layout. "Ditch your husband and come out with me and Alexis tonight. We haven't had a girl's night in forever."

"I'm sorry. I would, but Ryan and I have plans."

"Again?"

Bri laughed. "Well, tonight we're just going to watch a few movies and lay low."

And probably put all their pent up sexual tension to work. It sounded like a great night. She should have been happy that her friend was happy. Instead, Bri's plans only drove home the fact she *didn't* have plans with Drew.

"Why are you having a girl's night? I would have thought you'd be spending more time with Drew."

Hell, that's what Avery would have thought, too. Last night things had gone so well, and this morning everything seemed…off. There was nothing wrong with what he'd said during their phone call, exactly, but his whole tone had been filled with tension. Plus, he'd been shorter with her than she would have expected after how he'd held her while they fell asleep in each other's arms.

Maybe that was just her projecting, though.

She cleared her throat. "He had to work."

"That's too bad. You two seem to be getting pretty cozy, though. Things are going well?"

If by 'well,' Bri meant that they had spiraled out of control, then sure. She couldn't just laugh it off though, no matter how much she wanted to. "It's more difficult than I expected."

"These things always are."

Maybe, but Bri didn't have to be so goddamn smug about it. "It's fine."

"Of course it is. And so is the way Drew looks at you."

Her heart skipped a beat. "What?"

"Come on, you have to know he watches you like…I don't even know—like one of the heroes in my books watches the heroine."

"Wow, thanks for that enlightening comparison."

"You know what I mean. I think he *really* cares about you."

That didn't help her stress level any. It was just one more indication of how things were changing between the two of them. If *Bri* was noticing it, then they were in serious trouble.

But she already knew that.

Avery took a deep breath. "We'll have to do lunch

sometime, just the two of us. It feels like we haven't hung out without the guys in ages."

"Yeah, we'll definitely do that," Bri said. A male voice sounded in the background, asking if she'd already ordered the pizza. "I have to go. I'll call you later."

"Sure." She set her phone down and stared at the table she'd just spent an hour arranging. It wasn't right. With a curse, she grabbed all the items from its surface and tossed them behind the front desk.

Then she glared at her phone. Drew wasn't going to call and magically have the evening free. He was working a double, so he'd be plenty busy, and no doubt he wasn't spending much time obsessing about things he couldn't change.

Not like she was.

It was a good thing she had tonight to look forward to, or she'd be bound to do something stupid like call him again, just to hear his voice.

No. She'd go out and have fun with her sister and it would be enough. She would *not* call Drew and beg him to come over after his shift. No matter how Bri thought he looked at her.

She was better than that. She had to be.

• • •

"This is such a bad idea, I don't even know where to start." For what felt like the twenty-seventh time today, Avery called herself a freaking idiot. Girl's night out sounded like a great plan—right up until she and Alexis walked into the bar and she realized she couldn't have a drink.

"You needed to blow off some steam." Alexis shrugged

and flagged down the super cute bartender. The Matterhorn was a new bar in the outskirts of Williamsport that didn't seem to be able to make up its mind on what it wanted to be. There was a definite Belgian theme to the place—if you ignored the countless bras hanging from the chandeliers, lights, and pretty much every available space. The old school country music twanging from a beat up jukebox in the corner, and the pool tables littering the open space around the scattering of tables, should have clashed with the feel of the place—not to mention the Wheel of Good Drinks and Bad Ideas—but somehow it all came together into a cohesive whole.

Under different circumstances, that wheel might have been made for her.

"I can't drink." She didn't even *want* to at this point.

Alexis gave her a sympathetic look. "That's okay. I can drink for both of us. You'll dance and play pool and we'll just hang out. No drama and no worries. Sound good?"

It sounded perfect. If she could stop thinking about a certain guy who may or may not be falling as hard for her as she was for him. "I don't know how great company I'm going to be tonight."

"It'll be fine. We'll just be two little rays of sunshine together." Alexis gave her a side hug and then waved at the bartender. "I'd like an Appletini. My sister wants a Sprite."

"God, Alexis, take away all my fun." She leaned around her sister. "I'll have a Coke."

"You're really living on the edge with all that caffeine."

She laughed. They accepted their drinks and turned to face the rest of the bar. "So, since I'm living vicariously through you tonight, what's up first? Table dancing? Going to make out with a complete stranger? Maybe add your bra to the collection they have going up there?" She pointed at the ceiling.

Alexis crossed her arms over her chest. "Absolutely not. Do you know how much a Victoria Secret bra costs? I'm not making good enough money to just toss fifty bucks at a bar ceiling."

She sipped her Coke and couldn't stop herself from wishing there was some rum thrown in there. Her gaze flitted over the occupied pool tables before landing on the wheel. "This place is seriously something."

"It is." Alexis focused on the Wheel of Good Drinks and Bad Decisions, her eyes narrowing in a way that made the small hairs on the back of Avery's neck stand on end. "I'm going to do it."

"Do what?" Even as she asked, she had a feeling she knew.

Sure enough, her sister nodded at the giant wheel at the end of the bar. "That. I'm going to do it. Right now." She marched over, leaving Avery to trail behind her.

There was a faded paper with the rules written in marker—pay four dollars and do whatever the wheel says to get a shot of your choice. Four bucks for a shot was a pretty damn good deal. Then she looked at the actual wheel. Some of the options didn't seem so bad. Take a shot of top shelf liquor... Okay, well, that one actually seemed like a good thing.

But she didn't like the feverish glint in her sister's eyes one bit. "This isn't a good idea."

"Come on, live a little. I'll just do it a few times…"

"Once." She purposefully went with the minimum, hoping her by-the-books sister would take a hint.

She didn't. "Five times." Alexis pointed at one of the wedges. "Kiss a stranger. That could be fun."

Avery saw the night going sideways as she watched. "How about we go with a respectable three?" Her sister wasn't a big drinker, but she should be able to manage three shots. Avery would just have to make sure she ended up with some kind of watered down drink afterwards.

Alexis waved down the bartender. "Three turns of the wheel, please."

He raised a pierced eyebrow. It was a perfect match for the hoop circling his bottom lip. "You sure you don't want to try one and dip your feet in first?"

Avery nodded. That was a good point. "That sounds smart. Let's just start with one."

"Three turns." Alexis leaned her elbows on the bar. "Go big or go home, right?"

She eyed her sister's empty drink, wondering if she was making a terrible mistake by encouraging this. Alexis hadn't exactly been even-keeled lately, and the news about the potential baby didn't help matters. Throwing alcohol into the mix might be lighting a fuse on a keg of gunpowder.

She watched Alexis out of the corner of her eye. She was *grinning*. Maybe she had things backwards and letting loose for a while was *exactly* what her sister needed to get her mind off things.

God, she hoped so.

At least she'd be here to keep an eye on Alexis and make sure she didn't get too crazy. "You know, we can just take our drinks—get you a new one first—and go sit and chat for awhile instead."

Her sister turned her hazel eyes on Avery. They both

looked more Chinese than white, but Alexis had gotten Mom's eyes. For the first time, she saw exactly how much pain she carried around on a daily basis. It was staggering. "Alexis, I—"

"I'm tired of being good and respectable and doing everything right. Do you know what *Yé-ye* said to me today when he called? That he and *Nâinai* wouldn't turn their backs on me, despite the fact that I'm a bigger disappointment than Dad ever was. He said that at least I have an 'acceptable' job, so I wasn't a complete embarrassment." Alexis gave a choked laughed. "I graduated top of my class and work sixty hour weeks saving peoples' lives and it's *acceptable*. So, no, I'm not going to play it cool tonight. I need to let off steam as much as you do." She grabbed the cash out of Avery's hand and thrust it at the bartender. "Let's make it an even five."

Oh shit. Tonight just took a turn towards complete clusterfuck.

The bartender laughed. "Lady, I like your style."

The last time Alexis drank destructively was right after her ex-fiancé left. They'd almost ended up in jail. If it weren't for the cop who recognized Avery as Drew's best friend, they *would* have.

Drew.

She watched her sister spin the wheel, and pulled out her phone. Her chances of convincing Alexis to go home now were absolutely nil. Three shots was one thing, but five in such a short time? She was so screwed it wasn't even funny. Five shots from now, Alexis was going to be completely belligerent.

Avery could handle it, right? She didn't need to call in

reinforcements. As she turned her phone over in her hands, it felt a lot like she was looking for an excuse to talk to him. Besides, he was working tonight. It wasn't like he could drop everything and come, even if he wanted to.

Then the bartender did something she couldn't see and his voice projected from the speakers around the room. "Ladies and gents, I'd like to introduce you to Alexis. She's going to dance for her shot and she's chosen "Cherry Pie" as her song." He held out a hand and helped her sister up onto the bar as men and women around the room moved closer.

As the first few lines of the song started, Alexis raised her hands above her head and started to move. Once upon a time, she'd wanted to be a dancer—before their mother died and their world fell apart—and she still had the moves to prove it. Then one of the guys raised a handful of dollars and her sister got a dangerous grin on her face—the one that meant serious trouble.

Shit, shit, shit.

She dialed Drew. Texting would have been safer, but she needed to make sure he realized how vital his coming into town was.

And, goddamn her, she wanted to hear his voice.

"Avery, now isn't really a good…" He trailed off. "Why is "Cherry Pie" playing in the background?"

She said the three little words guaranteed to bring him running. "I'm in trouble."

He was quiet so long, she was suddenly afraid that they really *had* pushed things so far beyond repair that he wouldn't come for her when she needed him. It was amazing how much that thought hurt.

But when he spoke, he was all business. "Where are

you?"

"The Matterhorn. It's outside Williamsport on I-99." She looked over to where Alexis now twirled her shirt around her head. Yes, her white bra covered all the essentials, but this was not the buttoned-up sister she knew. "And Drew… Hurry."

Chapter Fourteen

Drew tore out of town, a thousand scenarios playing through his head. He couldn't remember the last time Avery had called him for help, and she'd sounded really worried over the phone. This wasn't just her getting drunk and needing a ride. This was something else.

God damn it. If he hadn't lied to her about working a double, she would have been with *him*, instead of out getting into whatever trouble she was in now. Stupid of him to let his issues get in the way of her safety, but how was he supposed to know she'd head out for a goddamn night on the town?

Not sure what to expect, he pulled up to the curb near the bar and parked. Nothing seemed to be on fire and there was no crowd rioting into the streets, but that wasn't nearly as comforting as he'd like it to be, not when he knew all too well how quickly things could spiral out of control without any outward warning.

He flashed his ID at the bouncer and walked into

complete chaos. Alexis was on the bar, wearing only her pants and a bra, dancing in a way most strippers *wished* they could move. He shouldered between two guys staring with their jaws on the ground.

Alexis leaned forward, giving the crowd near the bar a generous eyeful of cleavage, and that was when he caught sight of Avery. She actually looked panicked, and seemed to be pleading with her sister.

He made his way to their side in time to hear. "But, Avery, it's two hundred dollars if I hook it on the chandelier. This bra is only worth fifty." Alexis weaved on her feet, which would be a lot less dangerous if she wasn't standing on the bar in an impressively high set of heels. He hadn't even known she owned heels.

"Yeah, but I think your self respect is worth more than that."

"It's time to go home, girls."

Avery looked so relieved, he thought she'd throw herself into his arms. Alexis… Not so much. She shook her head. "I have one spin left."

"Spin?"

"The wheel." Avery pointed at a giant wheel at the end of the bar. "I'm going to kill that thing with fire the first chance I get."

He scanned the rules. "How many times?"

"She's on her eighth—and half of them have been her on the bar, dancing to 80's stripper songs."

He could hardly reconcile his view of Alexis with the woman grinning and hopping off the bar. She stumbled and, instantly, three guys moved up to "help." The glare he gave them sent them running. "It's time to leave."

"Not until I get my chance at two hundred dollars."

Knowing he was going to regret this, Drew asked, "How, exactly, do you win?"

"She's got to throw her bra up there and get it to stay." Avery pointed at the tiny chandelier at the highest point in the ceiling. "I told her it's impossible."

"And *I* told *her* that I was varsity softball three years running. I can make that. Cake."

Maybe if she was sober, but no way in hell could she do it in her current state. More than that, taking off her bra meant she was going to be topless, and Drew suspected Alexis would die of embarrassment when she woke up tomorrow and realized a bar full of strangers had seen her half naked.

For his part, he'd just go ahead and die right now.

"Nope. We're going home. Right now."

"Yeah, Alexis, let's go. I think there's a cheeseburger with your name on it in the McDonald's drive-thru." From the tone of her voice, this was an argument she'd already had a few times tonight.

"No." Alexis ripped her arm out of her sister's grasp and reached behind her back. "I'm a freaking adult, and I'm going to do what I want."

Avery's eyes flashed, and Drew decided to step in before she did something crazy—like punch her sister into submission. Using her fists to solve a problem wasn't a tactic she'd resorted to since high school—and never against Alexis—but he still remembered how well she could throw a right hook. He slid between them and snagged Alexis's hands. "Time to go."

In order to avoid another pointless argument, he reached

down and tossed her over his shoulder. Alexis screeched, but Avery gave him a grateful look. Having her look to him for help, even let him sweep in to save the day, made him feel ten feet tall. She didn't ask for help that often, but he did his damnedest to be there when she actually needed him. Especially now that he was all too aware of how easily he could lose this.

Everything was fine until the bouncer nearly clotheslined him. "I don't think so, buddy."

"It's okay, I'm a cop."

The guy gave him an incredulous look. "Yeah, cause that's really going to be enough for me to let you cart off a half naked chick screaming to be let go."

As if on cue, she started shrieking louder. "Help! Somebody help! Kidnapping! Murder!" What the fuck was she drinking tonight? He'd never seen mild-mannered Alexis lose her perfect persona, let alone anything on *this* level.

Avery slid between him and the bouncer. "Hi! Remember me? I'm the one who came in with her. My sister has had a few too many, so we're going to take her home."

The bouncer seemed to swell up. "Listen, lady, I don't care if you came in with her or if she had her tongue down your throat two seconds ago. You're not taking her home to play some sick twisted sex games when she's screaming bloody murder."

Sick twisted sex games?

Avery's eyes got really wide. "Whoa, dude. You obviously have a seriously overactive imagination. Which is great—for you. For us, on the other hand, not so great. And, seriously, ew. That's my sister you're talking about." She might have been a whole lot more convincing if Alexis weren't hanging over his shoulder, still yelling for help.

"Keep talking, lady. I'm calling the cops."

There was a decent chance he could talk his way through this. Drew knew all the local cops, and most of those even liked him. All he had to do was explain what was going on and things would be fine. He opened his mouth to tell the bouncer to go ahead and call the cops, when Avery sighed. "I'd really hoped it wouldn't come to this."

Then she clocked the guy in the face and shoved him to the side. "Run!"

"*What the fuck, Avery*?" He had no choice but to follow her, Alexis over his shoulder like a sack of potatoes. Playing good friend to a drunk girl was one thing. This was something else entirely.

"Hurry up!" She veered around a corner, her dark hair flying behind her.

He was going to kick her ass as soon as they got home. He might be down for some crazy shit, but this was just stupid. Assaulting the guy, when Drew probably could have talked his way out of the situation, was uncalled for. Everything about this day had turned into one giant shitstorm.

He recognized the street they turned onto and picked up his pace until he could grab a fistful of her shirt. "My truck's this way."

Another turn later and they were at his Dodge Ram. Drew unlocked it and set Alexis down. "We're taking you home. Shut up and I'll even stop for food on the way."

Instead of running like he'd feared, she slumped against the side of the truck. "I don't feel so good."

"She pukes and you're cleaning it up." He spun on Avery. "And what the fuck was that? I had everything under control, and then you just go and punch a guy? How much have you had to drink to think that was a good idea?"

Alexis giggled. "Too much carbonation."

What the—?

Avery glared. "You know what? We don't need you. Let me just find my car and you can take your own ass home."

"Not a chance." He helped Alexis into the backseat and slammed the door before he turned back to her. "What the hell has gotten into you?"

"I don't need your judgment or your help." She shoved her hands through her hair. "God, look at us. I never should have agreed to your bullshit plan."

Drew wished he could agree, but even with all the insanity, he'd never take back what had happened between them. Staying away from her today had been hell, and he didn't have any more answers now than he had that morning, but he knew one thing without question—he wouldn't have done anything differently. "I know this hasn't been ideal in some ways, but I'm not sorry we did it."

She stopped short. "Really?"

"Yeah. Last night was…" He searched for a word that fit. "Perfect."

Sirens cut through the night, entirely too close for his liking. Avery must have shared the same thought. "Time to go." Either that, or she wasn't too eager to follow this conversation to its conclusion. It was hard to say with her.

"Yep." He climbed into the driver's seat and she ran around the front of the truck and jumped in on the passenger side. Drew wanted to peel out and get home as fast as he'd gotten there, but there was no reason to advertise that they were running from something.

So he pulled from the curb and slowly worked his way north, keeping an eye out for any cops or other kind of pursuit. The irony of being a cop and hiding from them wasn't lost on him. If Ryan found out, he'd never hear the end of it. And if he had to bail Drew out? Yeah, no thanks.

"She's passed out, so I think you can skip the drive-thru."

"Okay."

Avery was silent until they drove beyond the city limits and the highway was surrounded on both sides by dark fields and trees. "Drew?"

"Yeah?" He braced himself for her to follow up on what he'd said earlier, about not wanting to change anything between them. He didn't have a good answer—or a plan when it came to the future—but he'd stand by that.

She surprised him, though. "Where's your uniform?"

He looked down at his jeans and T-shirt, wondering why she was asking... Until the truth hit. He'd told her he was working a double today. It was only ten, too early for him to be done with his shift—there was no way he could talk his way out of it. "I can explain."

"If you had other plans, you should have just said something. You didn't have to lie. "

"It's not what you think." Though he wasn't sure what the hell she thought.

"Look, it's none of my business. And, frankly, I don't even want to know."

That stung more than it should. "If you would just let me—"

"Do what? Lie to me more? Thanks, but no thanks." She sighed. "Please take us home."

"Avery—" He cut himself off. What could he say? She

knew he'd lied to her earlier. And she was right. Lying more wasn't going to do a damn thing to help his cause. And, really, he didn't *want* to lie to her, but telling her the truth wasn't an option, either. He'd thought he needed space, but an entire day spent thinking and he was no closer to the answers he needed than he'd been when he'd woken up.

All he knew was that he'd do anything to keep Avery in his life—as his best friend or, maybe, as something *more*.

They finished the rest of the drive in a silence that pricked along his skin, growing worse with each passing minute. By the time he pulled up in front of her house, he was about to start running his mouth until he dug himself into a hole he'd never get out of. Anything to get her talking, even if it meant she was yelling at him.

He turned to say—aw, hell, he didn't even know what—when a gurgling sound came from the backseat. "I'm gonna be sick."

"Shit." Avery gave him one last unreadable look and then she was gone, opening her door and then getting her sister out of the truck. "See you around." She turned and made her way to her front door without looking back.

Chapter Fifteen

All evidence Avery found of her sister the next morning was a pile of folded blankets on her couch and a note. *Sorry I was such a mess last night. I promise I'll make it up to you.*

She set the paper down and shook her head. Her sister had nothing to apologize for. Okay, there was the almost flashing a crowd of strangers and then almost getting them arrested, but Avery might have had something to do with that last part, and "almost" only counted in horseshoes and hand grenades.

She could forgive a whole hell of a lot, though, because it was painfully obvious her plan to get pregnant had opened up a heart wound in her sister that had never quite healed. Not that she expected Alexis to just up and get over the blows she'd been dealt over the last few years—though apparently *Yé-ye* did. But she also hadn't realized how deep they went. It wasn't something Avery could fix, no matter how much she wanted to. She'd just have to be there for her sister in any way Alexis would let her.

She rummaged through her cupboard, looking for coffee. It was only when she stepped back that she remembered she had none.

"Why me?" She leaned against the counter and cursed. Even if she didn't have the day off, after yesterday she had no desire for another visit to the coffee shop. God only knew who Old Joe would try to pair her up with next.

Though, at this point, maybe she should just suck it up and let him have his matchmaking way. Anything had to be better than the pit that opened up in her stomach when she realized Drew had lied to her last night. And his jumping in immediately to say he could explain…

She was so goddamn stupid. She had really fallen into the trap of believing this thing between them was special, even if they were fighting tooth and nail to keep their friendship intact. She'd forgotten the terms they set up.

Drew only signed on to be the father of her child. He never once said that it would be anything beyond sex. And he'd proven himself time and time again to be an expert at compartmentalizing to keep his heart out of the equation.

Was it possible he was sleeping with someone else on the side?

No. He wouldn't. Would he? Drew used to be a playboy. She wasn't sure when his last indiscretion was because he'd stopped talking about the women he ran around with awhile back, and she'd never asked. It didn't matter—Wellingford talked. There had been a blonde just passing through not too long ago. Or maybe it was a brunette?

Why am I even thinking about this? Torturing herself with Drew's conquests, current or otherwise, wasn't going to do anything but depress her.

Because she was one of them now.

A knock sounded at her front door, and she debated not answering. The only people she'd actually want to see this morning would just walk in, and she wasn't sure she was up to dealing with religious door-to-doorers without her coffee. But whoever was on the other side knocked again, apparently having no intention of leaving her to suffer in peace.

With a sigh, she crossed her living room and opened the door. Drew leaned against the frame, looking deliciously rumpled in an old shirt, and with faint circles under his eyes. He held up a hand, as if he thought she'd actually slam the door in his face. "I come bearing gifts."

She pressed her lips together and tried to keep her roil of emotions from her expression. Actually, slamming the door in his face sounded like a really good idea right now. She wasn't ready to fully process the fact that he lied to her, let alone the potential *why* of it. "I don't want to see you right now."

Drew offered a coffee cup, just close enough for her to catch a whiff of the mouth-watering scent. "It's your favorite."

Damn it, the man knew all her weaknesses. But that didn't mean what he'd done yesterday was forgiven. "Why are you here?"

"I want a chance to explain."

"Explain how you ditched me, you mean."

He sighed. "I needed some time to think. It's not like I was out banging some other chick. I was sitting at home, dealing with some shit."

She froze. "Why would you even bring up the possibility

of someone else?"

"What?"

And now she was sounding like a jealous girlfriend. This day couldn't get any worse. "Not that it's any of my business. We didn't agree to be exclusive." She needed to stop talking. Right now.

His eyes went wide. "That's what you think?"

"Can you blame me?" She leaned against the doorframe, hating how the idea of him with someone else made her so crazy jealous. Even though she tried to keep the words in, she blurted out, "That isn't an answer, by the way."

"Christ, Avery, I wasn't with anyone else—I haven't been in months."

She bit her lip before she could ask about the blonde/brunette that had the Wellingford gossip mill tittering. Even if he was with someone a month ago, that was weeks before they started this thing. It was none of her goddamn business, no matter how much the knowledge stuck in her throat. Needing a distraction, she held out a hand. "Gimme."

He handed it over. "I'm sorry. Fuck, I'm sorry I put you in a position where you thought that."

Which was the problem. A tiger couldn't change his stripes, and she'd been living in a fantasy world where he could. Drew was—and always had been—a playboy. He wasn't going to change and she'd be an idiot to want him to try. "I shouldn't have asked."

"No, that's not what I meant." He scrubbed a hand over his face. "The truth is that I haven't touched another woman since April."

It took a long second for the month to resonate. She stared. "That's the month I got my test results back."

"Yeah."

Even the smell of the coffee wasn't enough to relieve the weight of reality on her shoulders. He was such a good goddamn friend, and she was screwing this up completely. *She* was the one who couldn't keep things inside the tidy little lines they'd created at the beginning of this, which meant the blame for almost ruining their friendship lay solely on her.

She forced herself to look at him. "We have to cut this off before it's too late." She just hoped to God it wasn't already too late. "We're not the same, and neither of us is going to change." He might be able to protect his heart, but she couldn't. If they stopped this now, she'd have a chance to get her head on straight. Time would take care of the rest. "I mean, if I'm already pregnant, then cool. If I'm not, then I'll just go with the original sperm donor I picked. No harm, no foul."

For a second, she thought he might argue with her, but he just nodded. "I care about you too much to risk our friendship."

"I feel the same way." This friendship was everything to her. Putting it at risk was one of the crappier decisions she'd made lately.

Drew cracked a smile, though it looked as forced as hers felt. "Does this mean you forgive me?"

"We ran from the cops last night. That binds us in a way no one can touch." She sipped her coffee and her eyes drifted shut. "But this works, too."

"Avery, I— Can you open your eyes while I'm talking to you?"

"This coffee is orgasmic and, therefore, trumps whatever you're about to say." She took another sip. "God, this is good."

"Look at me."

She opened her eyes, finding him a whole lot closer than she'd anticipated. *Whoa*. She took a step back and let him into the house.

"I'd like to just have a day where we can go back to how things were—you, me, and some games." He held up the bag, and she caught sight of a handful of movies and the distinctive green cases of Xbox games and blue ones for Wii.

"You want an 'us' day?" It was exactly what she needed right now—a reminder that this mess of sex hadn't damaged their friendship. Avery reached into the bag and pulled out a six-pack of cans. "What's this?"

He shifted, not quite meeting her gaze. "I did a little checking after you freaked out about the beer the other day. Turns out, caffeine in big doses isn't a good idea when you're pregnant. I know you're probably not yet, but it doesn't hurt to start thinking about these things. No one in their right mind would ask you to give up your coffee, so I figured you'd want to cut it from other places."

Her heart thumped so loud, she was half surprised he couldn't hear it. "You looked into baby stuff for me."

"No, I looked into pregnancy stuff for you." He shrugged, as if he hadn't just shifted her world on its axis. "I figured I'd head the next freak-out off at the pass, so I armed myself accordingly."

If anything, his trying to downplay it made her heart beat harder. "They say the first step is knowing your enemy."

He finally looked at her, his blue eyes more vulnerable than she could ever remember seeing them. He needed this day as much as she did, Avery realized. As out of sorts as she'd been over having things *wrong* between them, he must have been just as much so. She wasn't sure if that made her feel better or worse.

Then he smiled and the moment passed. "Hey, I remember when Bri, who's the nicest person either of us knows, nearly bit my head off when I made the mistake of bringing chicken into her house. I'm just trying to be prepared—like a Boy Scout."

She nodded, fighting to keep a straight face. "Forewarned is forearmed. Though you're no Boy Scout."

"I totally was."

"For like half a year. It doesn't count." She made a face. "Not that I'm complaining. Every Eagle Scout I know is a bit funky in the head."

"Like James? Last I'd heard, he took off to Philly with plans of train-hopping down to some nudist commune in Florida." They were silent for a moment, and Avery contemplated what the hell had gone wrong with the sweet boy she'd gone to school with, to push him into such a weird course of life. Eagle Scouts. Enough said.

Suffice to say if she had a boy, he wouldn't be joining the Boy Scouts.

She touched her stomach, letting herself wonder about the future. If she succeeded in getting pregnant, would it be a boy or a girl? Holy shit, what if she had *twins*? She jerked her hand away, afraid even the thought would be enough to push that concept into reality.

She looked at Drew, who'd done something so thoughtful to make up the clusterfuck of yesterday to her. Maybe they really *were* okay. It warmed her chest until she felt like she couldn't breathe past it. "What do you want to do first?"

"Ladies choice." He grinned.

She grabbed the video game. "I think I'll kick your ass in *Madden*, and then we can watch some *Dead or Alive*— though, seriously, you're so transparent with this movie choice."

He tried and failed to look shocked. "I'm sorry if you can't appreciate my superior movie taste, but that's not my problem."

She held up the cover. "Uh huh. This is straight T and A."

"There are some great actresses in that movie and I don't like you insinuating that I..." He finally broke down and laughed. "Come on, can you blame me?"

"I totally can, but I'm not going to. I love this movie." It was so cheesy and bad that it crossed the line back into being good.

"That's because you also have superior movie taste."

Avery dropped onto the couch and picked up the remote from the coffee table. "Now, fire up that game so I can kick your ass."

"Fat chance, Yeung. The only thing you're going to be doing to my ass is checking it out as I fly past you for a winning touchdown."

She grinned, her world finally feeling like it was back in balance. "We'll see, Flannery. We'll see."

• • •

Drew settled next to Avery, struck by how *right* this was. As much as part of him had wanted to argue with her deciding to stop this—and with her going back to the original plan of putting another man's baby inside her—he couldn't. She was right. Things had spiraled so far out of control that he didn't know which way was up anymore. If she could put their friendship first, then he could do what it took to get over his issues and do the same.

That didn't mean he was okay with this bullshit about seeing other people, though. Hopefully that feeling of possessiveness would pass with time. Christ, he hoped so. Otherwise, seeing her settle down was going to kill him by slow degrees.

Obvlious to his inner turmoil, Avery got her console up and running and handed him a controller. They went through the motions of setting up a game. The silence as they picked their team wasn't anything like the one in his truck last night. He'd gone home after that and tossed and turned all night, all the ways he'd fucked things up taking root in his mind. All he'd known was that he had to fix things before they became irreparable.

To show up here and have her take his joke about another woman so seriously...

Christ.

He'd told the truth. It had been months since he'd hooked up with anyone, since right before she got her testing shit back. And then Drew had done everything he could to be there for Avery while she worked through the turmoil the results brought. It hadn't been easy on either of them. The genetic markers might not be actual cancer, but he'd been by her side for both her mother's death and Alexis's ordeal. The thought of that happening to Avery was enough to have him waking up in a cold sweat. What was some piece of ass compared to that?

The more he thought about it, the surer he was that her decision to put them back into familiar territory was the right one. They had to stop this shit before he lost her for good. He forced a grin. "You ready?"

"I was born ready." She leaned forward as the game started, her thumbs flying over the buttons as she tried to run the football down the field.

He'd seen her use that play before, though, and he was prepared for her. Drew's defensive lineman tackled her quarterback and he whooped. "What's that I was hearing about you kicking my ass?"

"The day is young." She elbowed him. "I'm about to pull out my super secret weapon. You'll never see it coming."

"Your mouth keeps writing checks that your ass can't cash. Just like always."

"Always? Please. I'm reigning *Mario Kart* champion. No one can argue that."

He really couldn't since she constantly dominated during that game. Drew glanced at her, loving the way her dark eyes lit up with challenge. He grinned. "They're two different animals, young grasshopper, which you'll figure out soon enough." He refocused on the game in time to see her wide reciever catch a long pass and sprint into the end zone.

"What's that?" She jumped to her feet and cupped her hand around her ear. "I thought I heard you explaining how I'm not going to dominate this game." She laughed and did the Avery version of a touchdown dance—knees high and her arms pumping.

It was the most adorable thing he'd ever seen.

She paused, her arms dropping to her sides. "I feel like you're judging me right now."

"Avery—"

"You can explain it away however you want, but I know the truth. You're so filled with shame that you don't know how you'll get up in the morning." She held up a hand when he pushed to his feet. "It's okay, Drew. There will be other games. I'm sure you'll have your day in, say, about five years."

God, she was driving him crazy in the best way possible. "Five years? It was one touchdown."

"One in the long line of many future ones." She laughed. "Because I'm obviously superior in all things."

The sad truth was that she *was*. No one else could compare to her on any level, a fact which was only becoming clearer the longer this thing between them went on. Why would he have lied to her in order to take out another woman when all he wanted was *her*?

Avery opened her mouth—no doubt to deliver some more hilarious shit-talking—but Drew didn't give her a chance.

He pulled her against him and kissed her, reveling in the feel of her going soft against the front of his body. He dug his hands into her hair, tipping her head back so he could slant his mouth over hers, slipping his tongue between her lips.

She pulled away just enough to say, "I thought we were stopping."

"I changed my mind." Drew kissed her again, reaching down to dip his hand under the waistband of her sweats and squeeze her ass. "Christ, sweetheart, do you *ever* wear underwear?"

"I was sleeping." She worked his shirt over his head and dropped it on the floor.

He gave her a little push, guiding her to the couch.

"Down." While she was laughing, he wrestled off her sweats and shirt, leaving her naked.

She was so goddamn beautiful.

Avery, of course, didn't sit still long enough for him to look his fill—and he wasn't sure he *could* get his fill of her. She unbuttoned his jeans with deft fingers, shooting him a look through her lashes. "Hold still."

She worked his pants down his hips and took his cock in her hand, and he couldn't have moved if he wanted to. Being touched by her was too perfect, especially when she had that dangerous little smile on her lips. Intense Avery rocked his world, but a Mischevious Avery was devastating. She stroked him once, twice, three times.

"Avery, I—" She took him in her mouth, cutting off the rest of his words. He looked down at her, at the picture she made with her hair a tangled mess and her perfect pink lips wrapped around his cock, and it was everything he could do to keep his knees from buckling.

She circled her tongue around the head of his cock and dipped down, sucking him deep until he bumped the back of her throat. Then she looked up and met his gaze, bringing a startling intimacy to the whole encounter. She held his gaze as she worked him with her tongue and lips, her touch so intoxicating that he was in danger of coming right then and there. "Fuck."

"Hmmm?"

She had to know this was possibly the single hottest experience of his life—her giving him head in the middle of her living room with the morning light streaming through the windows. "Sweetheart, I need to touch you."

She let him go almost reluctantly and leaned back,

propping herself up on her elbows. "Someday, I'm going to finish you like that."

If she did, he'd never be the same. The irony was that while he'd been trying to ruin her for any other man, she'd gone and done the same for him and any future woman he might meet. Drew kicked off his jeans and went to his knees in front of her. He kissed her, stroking a hand down the front of her body to cup her between her legs. She was drenched, obviously having enjoyed that blow job nearly as much as he did. "Damn it, Avery. You're going to be my undoing."

• • •

His dangerous words hit her right in the chest, but she was too needy to stop and question him. It was too late, anyways. They'd reached the point of no return ages ago. So Avery dredged up a wicked grin. "Let's not talk anymore."

Before he could say anything else, she positioned him at her entrance and gasped when he worked into her with little strokes. This feeling, right here, right now, was completion. Had she ever felt like this with another person? She didn't think so.

No, that was a lie. She knew for a fact Drew was the only one to ever affect her on this level.

He hissed out a breath when he was finally sheathed completely. "Christ, sweetheart, I don't think I'm ever going to get enough of you."

Why did he have to?

The question was swept away and he spread her legs wider, draping them over his arms as he started to move. He drove into her, possessing her in a way no one ever had before, ripping cries from her throat as she dug her nails into his forearms.

"I need…" A frown flitted over his face, but then he moved her legs up to his shoulders, the new position giving him leverage to sink even deeper. "There. God, that feels good."

Good? Good didn't begin to describe the feeling soaring through her. She tried to move with him, but this position kept her entirely at his mercy.

And he had none.

Drew did something with his hips that stole her breath. He paused, and then did it again, his gaze pinning her in place as thoroughly as his body did. "You like that."

It wasn't a question, but the third time he rubbed over that spot deep inside her, she screamed. "Oh my God, *yes.*" Her orgasm hit her like a freight train, sucking her under and then throwing her back into reality as Drew shuddered over her. He slumped against her, having the presence of mind to shift her legs lower, but then he laid his head against her shoulder, his breath coming as harshly as hers.

Finally, Drew laughed. "On a scale of one to ten, I think that was at least a thirteen."

She wasn't sure there was a number large enough to encompass their sexual experiences together. Thirteen sounded good, though. "Definitely."

He lifted his head and kissed her. "Ready to get back to *Madden*?"

"If you're trying to distract me and throw me off my game, you win. You win it all."

"Sweetheart, I have you naked and in my arms. I *know* I win it all."

When he said things like that, it was all too easy to picture this being their new norm—games and joking and really hot sex. Drew collapsed on the couch and pulled her up to lean against his side. There was no rush for his clothes, no awkwardness, nothing but this wonderful comfort between them. She traced a single finger up the center of his stomach and stopped between his pecs. "*Yé-ye* called me yesterday. He wants me there for dinner tomorrow."

He laughed. "Your idea of pillow talk leaves something to be desired."

"I strive for excellence in everything I do." She smiled against his chest, though the expression didn't last. "It's time. I'm not ready to tell them, but it's time."

He gathered her tighter against him, his warm arms comforting even as he kissed her temple. "I'll pick you up at six-thirty."

"You don't have to." Even as she spoke, she was glad for his offer. Maybe it was cowardice, but the last thing she wanted was to face her grandparents alone and tell them she was procreating with someone who they'd never approve of.

"It has nothing to do with 'have to' and everything to do with 'want to.' I said I would be there for you, and I am."

How was she supposed to keep her head on straight with him holding her so closely and saying all the right things? They'd just decided to take things back to their norm, and that resolution had lasted all of fifteen minutes. And now he was saying all sorts of things to make her think that maybe Bri wasn't as crazy as she'd thought—that maybe *she* wasn't crazy for feeling the way she did. Avery lifted her head and kissed him. "In that case, thank you. I'd like for you to be there."

"Done." He shifted, setting her aside so he could sit up. "And now that that's taken care of, it's time for my comeback."

She laughed and pulled on his discarded shirt. It dwarfed her, but there was something wonderful about being covered in something of his. She grabbed the controller. "In your dreams, Flannery. Let's do this."

Chapter Sixteen

Drew's day consisted of breaking up an argument between the Diner's longtime waitress, Dorothy, and a pair of idiot high school freshman. Dorothy was mollified once she saw what he had planned for them—a ride down Main Street with the lights blazing and both boys in the backseat of his cruiser. They'd slunk lower with each person who'd seen them, knowing damn well that, with the Wellingford gossip mill, the news would get to their parents before they could.

But even that fun little detour wasn't enough to shake his feeling that he'd fucked things up beyond all recognition. Because all he could wonder while he was taking the boys down Main Street was if he'd be doing the same damn thing in sixteen years with his own kid.

Hell if *that* wasn't an unnerving thought.

After his shift was over, he headed home and showered in record time. He thanked God he'd actually gotten around to doing laundry since the last time he wore his slacks and nice shirt, so he had something suitable for dinner. Once he was dressed, he drove back into town and headed for Avery's. Even all the worries circling in his head weren't enough to dampen his need to see her again.

He was early, but that was for the best. Her grandfather already had enough ammo to make her miserable with—no need to add being late to it. Drew just hoped that his being there for this family dinner would be enough. He didn't like the idea of her being uncomfortable, especially when this wasn't something he could save her from. Assholes or not, her grandparents were still her family. He knew all too well how permanent family was, even when someone wished it didn't have to be.

Avery met him at the front door wearing a flowered sundress, her choice of clothing giving away more about her mental state than if she'd waved a giant flag shouting, "I'm nervous!"

She gave him a small smile as she slid into his truck, but he wasn't going to let her sit over there and stew the whole way. She needed a distraction now more than she needed time to think, so he snagged her elbow and towed her over to his side. "Hey there."

"Hey."

He draped his arm over the back of the seat. "How was your day?"

"Fine."

"How many times did you sneak off to the bathroom and think about me while you touched yourself?"

She made a choked noise and finally looked at him. "What?"

"It's a totally legitimate question. I know how insatiable

you are." It was one of the many things he'd discovered in the last week.

"That doesn't mean I can't go twelve hours without orgasm."

"Maybe you can, but you shouldn't."

She shook her head and laughed. "You're an idiot."

"But I'm awesome."

This time her laugh was a lot less forced. "Yeah, you're pretty awesome."

Drew fist pumped. "Victory."

They bickered playfully until he pulled into her father's driveway. Avery fell into silence, a frown on her face. "It's not too late to call the whole thing off. We can run away and join a traveling circus," she said.

"A traveling circus."

"Yeah. I'll tell fortunes and you can be the dancing bear."

He snorted. "Now you're just being mean. I can't grow a mountain man beard, let alone pass for a bear. Besides, I'm way too pretty for that shit."

"Seriously." She turned to face him fully, practically pleading. "Let's go into Williamsport. We can go eat some-where—anywhere. My treat."

"Sweetheart, you're going to have to tell them eventu-ally." He took her hand again, hating how cold it was. "It will be okay."

"I know I have to tell them eventually. Say, in like a year."

This wasn't the brash and outgoing woman he knew. Her grandparents had always brought out this side in her. She might not bend to the plans they had for her life, but her grandfather specifically seemed to have a knack for getting under her skin.

She shook herself. "Never mind. You're right. Let's do this shit."

"That's the spirit. Give 'em piss and vinegar."

She made a face. "I don't think that's how the saying goes."

"Prove it." He had her focusing on anything but walking through the front door, which was what he'd been aiming for. Drew got out of the truck and held the door open so she could follow him. He offered his hand, and she took it with a real smile, hanging on tightly as they walked up the driveway and to the front porch. Thankfully, it was her dad who answered. Avery's smile lost some of its shakiness. "Hey, Dad."

"Hey, honey." He stepped back so they could walk through the door. "Drew."

"Mr. Yeung."

He shook his head. "After all these years, I believe it's okay for you to call me Sheng."

They'd been having this conversation ever since Drew and Avery graduated high school, but he'd never been able to make the shift. Tonight wouldn't be the night he started, either. Plus... "I don't think your parents would be okay with that."

Sheng sighed. "They haven't quite caught up with the changing world."

There were blatant tension lines around Avery's mouth that he wished he could kiss away. As much as she was so obviously dreading it, she could do this. She was too strong to be pulled from her path just because of some intense disapproval from family members she hadn't even met until she was in junior high.

As they followed Sheng down the hall towards the dining room, Drew leaned in close to Avery. "Time to put your game face on."

"I was born with my game face on."

"I know." He smiled. "Just remember, however they react, I'm here for you."

"Thanks, but I got this."

The formal dining room had been set, complete with china plates and candlelight. Avery's grandfather sat at the head of the table and, once again, Drew had a hard time reconciling this wizened old man with the tyrant who tried to run both the girls' lives. He peered up through thick black spectacles, a frown creating a sea of wrinkles along his forehead. "Who's this, now?"

"*Yé-ye*, I brought a guest. You remember Drew Flannery."

"That loud boy who likes to climb trees?" It was the same song and dance they always had since the unfortunate event that introduced Drew to Avery's grandfather. Even though he knew it was the old man's way of trying to put him in his place, it still set his teeth on edge.

"The very one."

He somehow managed to look down his nose at Drew, despite being five-foot-nothing *and* sitting down. "I suppose that's fine. Your sister has decided not to grace us with her presence, so we have an extra setting."

He couldn't blame Alexis. Her grandfather barely managed to be civil to Avery—some of the time. He didn't even bother with Alexis anymore. It blew Drew's mind. How the hell did her worth as a person boil down to marrying a

Chinese man and having his babies? Most families would have been tickled pink to have a child who grew up to be a nurse like Alexis had. Apparently that wasn't good enough for Mr. Yeung.

The door leading to the kitchen opened and Meiling tottered in, balancing a tray of shredded pork with vegetables. Drew rushed over and plucked it from her hands. "Let me help."

She blinked at him. "Drew Flannery. What a delight."

For all her sweet voice and grandmotherly looks, she could be just as much a hard ass as her husband. But she made cookies, so she was all right in his book. "Where would you like this?"

Meiling gestured to the center of the table and he obediently set it there. Then Sheng came through the door with the last of the food and they all took their seats. They ate in silence, which had always bugged Drew on the rare times he was invited to dinner. He might live alone, but he hated the quiet like this, filled with tension and unspoken things. It reminded him all too clearly of the same silence that had filled his house growing up—the one he and Ryan tried their damnedest not to break, because the alternative was to be faced with an angry, hungover bastard.

Those were the times when he'd tow Ryan out of the house on some errand or adventure. More often than not, they ended up in trouble of some sort, but it was worth it not to have to worry about what bullshit Billy would come up with if they woke him before he'd slept off his drunk.

He made an effort to shake off the past and followed Avery's lead. This was her dog and pony show. He was only supposed to be here for emotional support.

And to keep her from going for her grandfather's throat when he invariably said something cutting and unforgivable.

• • •

Dinner ended, the food melding together into a solid block in Avery's stomach. It was now or never. "I have something to tell you."

Nâinai had started to stand—no doubt to clear the table—but she sat. "What is it, *Sunnu*?"

Avery took a hasty drink of water—and nearly jumped out of her skin when Drew's hand closed around her knee under the table, offering his silent support. She could do this. She wasn't going to chicken out and flee for the nearest exit. "I've decided to have a baby."

A terrible silence descended on the room. Dad, at least, didn't look ready to put her head on a chopping block. *Yé-ye* was a different story altogether. "Excuse me?"

"I've been informed by my doctor that I have the same genetic markers both Mom and Alexis did, and as a precaution, he highly recommends the procedure they had to do for both of them. Since I know that will take away my ability to have biological children, I've decided to have one before then."

Yé-ye turned to Dad and switched to Chinese. "This is your fault, Sheng. If you hadn't married that woman—"

"*Fu!*"

"Enough." Avery was surprised at the strength of her voice, but she had to make her grandfather stop talking before he truly said something unforgivable. It was common enough knowledge that he and *Nâinai* had never approved of Mom, but he'd never gone so far as to blame her for all their troubles. She wouldn't stand for it.

She took a deep breath and kept going. "This genetic abnormality could happen to anyone. Stop blaming my mother."

"It came from *her* side of the family." *Yé-ye* patted his lips with his napkin, apparently unconcerned about the emotional health of anyone else at the table. "I had thought we were past this business when she died, but then Alexis went and took such dramatic means."

Avery could almost feel the anger raising her temperature. "My sister did what she had to in order to live. That's not dramatic."

Yé-ye turned dark eyes faded with age her way. "And look where that ended, Avery. With her respectable fiancé leaving her, and her ability to continue the family line taken away."

"*Yé-ye*—"

He continued talking like she hadn't said a damn thing. "We'd had such high hopes for you, and now you're indulging in this unnatural process."

The roaring in her ears nearly drowned out her grandfather's angry words and *Nâinai*'s trying to calm everyone down. All she could see was her grandfather and the judgment he wielded like some sort of gavel. He wanted something to judge? Well, she was going to give it to him. "I think two people coming together to make a baby is hardly unnatural. It's the most natural thing in the world."

Drew's hand spasmed on her knee, but there was no taking back the words. It was almost a relief to see the color rise to *Yé-ye*'s face. "What did you say?"

"That's the last part of my news." She grabbed Drew's hand and brought it to her lips. "Drew and I are having a baby."

"*No*. I will not allow it." Her grandfather stood, nearly knocking his chair over. "This cannot go on."

"It's too late to worry about it now."

"Bad enough for you to take these matters so far, but to do it with *him*." *Yé-ye* looked like he wanted to spit. "I knew you were rebellious, Avery. I never knew you were a whore."

Just like that, all the blood rushed out of her head, leaving her weaving in her seat. Had her grandfather just called her a whore? In front of everyone, which shouldn't have mattered and yet somehow did? Dad and *Nâinai* fell into shocked silence, as if they couldn't quite believe it either.

Drew went tense beside her. "I don't know. I hardly think Avery having sex with the man she's going to marry makes her a whore."

Marry? What the fuck was he talking about? She spun to face him. "I'm not marrying you."

"Sure you are." He gave her a lazy wink, and then turned back to *Yé-ye*. "She's being stubborn, but I plan on making an honest woman of her."

"Get out." Her grandfather pointed a shaking finger at the door. "Get out of this house, both of you. You are no longer welcome here."

Avery pushed to her feet on legs she wasn't sure would hold. "That suits me just fine. If you decide to pull your head out of your ass in time to see the only great-grandchild you'll ever have, give me a call." Then she stormed out of the room, moving as quickly as she could, because it felt like the world was shattering around her ears.

Even knowing her grandfather wouldn't be pleased, she hadn't expected him to react like *that*. She should have known better. This was the same man who'd cut off all contact with his only son after Dad married her American mother. How much more likely was he to do it to a granddaughter who wasn't even fully Chinese?

It still hurt. More than she could have expected.

Her dad's voice stopped her. "Avery, wait."

She stopped just outside the front door, gripping Drew's hand like it was a lifeline. Hell, it pretty much was. If her father turned away from her right now, she was going to lose it. Still, she kept her chin high and her shoulders back as she turned to face him. Show no fear. Give your enemies nothing. It was the only lesson *Yé-ye* ever taught her that she held close to her heart.

Dad shut the door behind him. In the faint light of the porch, she couldn't read any expression on his face. "Avery... I'm proud of you, honey." He broke off, and took a shuddering breath. "And I know your mom would be, too."

With a sob, she let go of Drew's hand and threw herself into her father's arms. "Thank you, Daddy." When was the last time she called him that? She couldn't remember.

He hugged her tightly for a moment before holding her shoulders and taking a step back. "I can't promise he'll come around, but I'll be here." Dad pressed a kiss to her forehead and looked at Drew. "If you break my daughter's heart, I will have no problem breaking both your kneecaps."

Even considering the threat came from a man who barely reached his shoulder, Drew still paled. "Yes, sir."

"Now get out of here. Go do something to wash the bad taste of dinner away."

"We will, sir." He reclaimed her hand and tugged her down the porch steps. With one last look at her father, she turned and walked with Drew to the truck. He held the door open for her and then crossed around to his side.

She pressed her hands to her cheeks, as if that would do something to stem the flow of tears. There was too much, too many emotions coursing through her right now for her to win that battle.

At least she hadn't cried in front of *Yé-ye*.

Drew started the truck. "I think that went well."

"Oh yeah?" She laughed, the watery sound making her cringe. "I do not think that word means what you think it means."

"If you can quote *The Princess Bride* at me, then you're going to be okay." He pulled her into the middle of the bench seat and draped his arm over her shoulders. There was nothing sexual in the move—just comfort. "Your grandpa is a dick, but we knew that going in."

"Doesn't make it any easier knowing I've been crossed out of pretty much every family gathering from now until the end of time."

"I think your grandma might have a thing or two to say to him once they get alone."

"What do you mean?" She laid her head on his shoulder, letting her guard down for the first time since they'd pulled into her dad's driveway.

"You were too busy yelling at him to see her face, but when you mentioned a great-grandbaby and he commanded you out of the house, she looked ready to take a two-by-four to the side of his head. I don't think she's going to let him stand in the way of her having a relationship with the kid."

"You don't know my grandparents. They cut off communication from Dad for *fifteen years*."

"And I bet that nearly tore out Meiling's heart." He squeezed her shoulder. "Maybe it won't happen, but I wouldn't place bets against the woman."

"You just say that because you like her cookies." She crossed her arms over her chest. "And what the hell was that about me marrying you? That's bullshit and you know it."

His mouth tightened. "Yeah, sure."

That was a non-answer if she ever heard one. "Why, Drew?" His answer mattered a whole hell of a lot, because even if it was crazy in a huge way, it still signaled a deeper meaning.

Unless he was totally and completely talking out of his ass.

When had her life gotten so complicated? She almost laughed at the thought. Oh yeah, when she agreed to let her best friend help her get pregnant the old fashioned way. She sat back in the seat and closed her eyes. "Never mind. I don't want to know. Just take me home, please." Anything to get away from the tight confines of his truck cab and his overwhelming presence.

• • •

Drew hated how small she felt against him. If he took her home, he could hold her while she tried not to cry, but at the thought of that, he felt a helpless kind of fury rise in him that he'd never be able to act on. He hadn't helped at dinner tonight. In fact, he was pretty sure he'd made things worse by blurting out that they were getting married.

Her reaction sure as hell hadn't been happy.

What the fuck was I thinking?

Oh yeah, he'd been thinking that he'd do whatever it took to wipe that lost look off her face. It didn't matter that marriage was one of the things that he'd promised himself he'd never do. Look what happened to his old man. Letting someone that close was just asking to have your heart ripped out and served to you on a platter. Except Avery was *already* that close. If nothing else, this whole thing had brought that into perspective.

And he was going to lose her.

Maybe it wouldn't be to cancer, but he'd lose her all the same if she went on with this plan she had for her life. She fully intended to marry someone else, to raise his child with someone else, to build a life *with someone else*. Which would leave Drew as a permanent outsider, like a kid on a cold street peering through a window at a life he could never have.

So which was worse? Having her and potentially losing her the way his old man lost his mom? Or never taking that step and always being kept at a distance?

If he did this, if he married her, he'd never have to lose her. Not like that.

He glanced at the clock on his dashboard twice before the numbers registered. Twenty to ten. Perfect timing. He squeezed Avery's shoulders. "Want to know what we need right now?"

"What's that?"

Words from their childhood rose, words he hadn't spoken in over ten years. "An escape."

She twisted against him, lifting her head to meet his

gaze. Whatever she saw on his face made her jaw drop. "We haven't done that since we graduated high school."

They hadn't needed to. Or, if that wasn't strictly true, neither of them had brought up the old escape route they'd used so many times that they'd beaten down a trail. Well, they needed it now. Desperately. He'd had *one* job—all he had to do was be there to offer support if she needed him. The messed up truth was that she *hadn't* needed him. There'd been no good goddamn reason for him to jump in with the marriage thing other than hating how her grandfather talked to her.

Oh, yeah, and the fact that he didn't want her to be with anyone else.

But that didn't mean he was ready to lock down a life with her, either. Shit, what was he even thinking? This was insane. And the way she shut him out when she asked him to take her home...

He couldn't let her shut him out.

He turned back to the road. "We need it."

He floored it out of town, taking the turn that would lead up to Billy's old place. Technically, it was his now. He'd bought out Ryan's half under the excuse that he wanted to do some repairs to the house, with the promise to his brother to look into reselling. His brother had been more than happy to be rid of the place.

Drew hadn't set foot in it since he cleared it out after Billy died eight years ago.

He kept telling himself that he'd take the winding dirt road up to the house, if only to burn the motherfucker to the ground. But he never had. He couldn't bring himself to face the memories it held, to stand against the past rushing into him and chasing away the distance he'd fought so hard for.

They didn't go to the house tonight. Instead, he pulled his truck into the little turnoff at the first curve and put it in park. "Ready?"

"Always." Again, their usual question and answer. It didn't give him the peace it used to, but he wouldn't need this escape if he were already in his right mind.

He opened the door and they both climbed out the driver's side and stood at the gap between two trees, where their path was. The years had given it back to the forest, but there was still plenty of space. In the distance, a train blew its whistle. "Come on." He took her hand and they ran, the weeds whipping at their legs, the breeze of their passing creating a flag of Avery's hair behind her.

They hit the top of the hill just as the engine came around the bend. He dropped onto the cleared spot and she did the same next to him. Each train car that passed seemed to take him further back in time—and away from his current problems—replaying all the times they'd snuck out here at night to get away from their lives.

First it was just Drew. He'd wait until he was sure Billy was passed out, until Ryan could sleep without worrying about their father, and then he'd run down here and scream out his frustration and pain, where the rumble of the tracks and the shriek of the whistle drowned him out, no matter how loud he was. Here, he was insignificant and he could yell himself hoarse, and it changed nothing. No one depended on him, and he could let down the mask he fought so hard to keep during the day to protect Ryan.

He brought Avery out here the night they found out her mom's cancer came back. She hadn't cried, hadn't screamed, had just sat in the same spot she was now, and stared at the train as if it held all the answers of the universe.

Just like she was right now.

They'd been here so often, but he'd never let himself scream in front of her. Hell, he hadn't *needed* to once he shared this place with her. They were just two people, embroiled in their own pain, both needing the escape the night and the sound of the train brought.

All too soon, it passed, leaving only the faintest rumble as the last car rounded the bend and headed off into the darkness. It hadn't changed anything, hadn't solved a single one of his fuckups, but for those few short minutes, he'd had a clear head and no worries. That alone was priceless.

In the new silence, Avery leaned against his shoulder. "Some days I wish I could hate him. It would be so much easier if I could hate him."

It was like she'd pulled the thought directly from his head. Life would be simpler if it were truly black and white, if he could look at the piece of shit Billy had been and hate him for neglecting his boys and putting them through hell. And there *was* hate in there some days. He hated what the man had turned into. He hated that Billy had loved Mom so consummingly that he hadn't been strong enough to hold it together after she died, hadn't been there for them when he and Ryan needed him the most.

But he looked at Avery and tried to picture what he'd do if she disappeared from his life—*truly* disappeared—and in that moment he could understand only too well what that kind of loss could do to a man.

Chapter Seventeen

Drew stopped in front of Avery's house and shut off his truck. He hadn't been able to shake the memories clinging to him in the fifteen minutes it had taken to get there, and he didn't see that changing anytime soon. But he also couldn't leave her in her own personal hell tonight. Not after the way he'd failed her at dinner.

No matter what shitty company he was right now. "Can I come in?"

She gave him a strange look. "Uh, yeah. Baby or not, I need a beer after that mess." She sighed. "God, I can't do that. I'm so angry and upset, I can't see straight, and I can't even wind down with a beer. And now I feel like an ass for even bitching about it."

"After that dinner, you're entitled to a little bitching." He followed her to the front door, and turned to look at her street while she got out her keys.

It was quiet, each small house sitting back on perfectly

manicured lawns. A little ways down the street, he caught sight of Miss Nora Lee walking her beast of a dog. The little old woman had been walking the neighborhoods of Wellingford since he was a kid, though she used to have two mastiffs back then. He'd always suspected it was part of the reason she knew all the best gossip—because she was scouring the streets for it. Now it was only Brutus dogging her heels. She waved as she passed, though thankfully she didn't stop to chat.

This was a good street—a good place to raise a kid—but he couldn't help wondering if it wasn't better to go even further outside town. Somewhere the kid could run free without having to worry about even slow moving drivers, where there were endless acres to be explored and adventures to have.

Somewhere more like his place.

God, what was he thinking? Damn it, he couldn't even pretend anymore. He'd been toying with the idea in the back of his mind ever since they babysat Lily—of being more than a favored uncle who was forced to sit back and let another man step in as father.

Of actually *being* that father.

He dropped onto Avery's couch and wondered if he'd finally lost his mind. Then she turned to him with *that* look on her face, and he knew he had. He shoved to his feet as she took a step forward. "Come on." He might not know what he was going to do with the future that had dropped into his lap, but he knew one thing for sure—Avery was in it. Right now, his best friend needed him.

And he needed her, too.

When they reached the doorway to her room, he pulled

her into his arms. She felt good there. Right. As she slipped her arms around his neck and melted against him, he was on thin ice and slipping fast. He couldn't imagine his life like it used to be, before he was able to pull her into his lap and do whatever it took to make her cry out his name. Before he had the ability to hold her as they fell asleep at night.

If I married her, I'd get that every night.

Drew kissed her, doing his damnedest to drive each and every thought out of both their heads. She arched against him, and the feel of her body made him want to tear off both their clothes so they could be skin to skin. He reached down and lifted her dress, barely breaking the kiss long enough to pull it over her head. Her hands were already at his belt buckle, so he went ahead and yanked off his shirt and pulled her back into his arms.

There. That was so goddamn good.

He maneuvered her to the bed and lowered her onto it, needing to show her the emotion he couldn't quite bring himself to put into words. But he could do it with touch, with his hands on her skin, with his mouth against hers, with the feeling of wrapping her up because he never wanted to let her go. He propped himself up on his hands and drank in the sight of her beneath him.

Fuck, she was gorgeous, though her body couldn't compare to the look in her eyes as she dragged her gaze over him. As if she couldn't get enough of looking at *him*. He could barely dare hope that she wanted him as much as he wanted her—that she wanted the same things he did.

She hooked the back of his neck. "Get down here."

Instead of covering her like they both wanted, he lay down next to her and trailed his hand over her skin. He stopped just short of her panties and dragged his thumb under the edge of the cotton. "Tonight we're taking our time."

· · ·

Avery was already nodding before he finished talking. "Okay." After the nightmare of dinner with her family, she needed escape as much as she needed her next breath. His taking her to their old hiding place had helped, but Drew touching her like *this* did more than help. It freed her to be right here, in this moment, and let her worries go.

They would still be there tomorrow.

He slipped his hand into her panties and her mind blanked completely. As he cupped her, words tried to get past her lips, words she had no business thinking, and sure as hell had no business saying aloud. She pressed her heels into the mattress, lifting her hips in a silent demand that he seemed more than happy to respond to. He slid two fingers into her and, with his hand trapped close to her skin by her panties, it felt too possessive to put into words.

She loved every second of it.

He kissed her lips, her jaw, her neck, each touch damn near reverent. All while working her with his fingers. Drew's breath rasped in her ear. "Tonight…"

She bit her lip. "Yeah?"

"Tonight isn't for the baby. This is just you and me."

Before she could come up with a response—a response beyond almost coming on the spot—he worked his way down her body and shoved off her panties. Then it was only his mouth on her and his words ringing in her ears. The feeling of his whiskers against her thighs and his tongue dragging over her nearly sent her over the edge. "Drew!"

"That's right, sweetheart. Come for me."

Her body wound tighter and tighter as he sucked her clit into his mouth, his teeth gently raking over the sensitive bundle of nerves. She dug her fingers into his hair, desperate to get him closer. "That feels so good."

He lifted his head despite her grip and looked her in the eye. What she saw there shocked her to the core. There was a healthy dose of lust in those blue eyes, but there was also something else altogether—something both dark and soft at the same time.

Something that looked a lot like love.

Before she could really process it, he crawled up her body and kissed her. His tongue slid along hers as he settled between her thighs, and she decided she could worry about things later. Right now it was just him and her, with nothing between them. He shifted and then his cock was there, pressing against her entrance, ready to claim her completely.

She wrapped her legs around his waist, needing him there, as close as he could get. This was real. He framed her face with his hands. "Can I stay tonight? All night?"

"Yes." She wanted this feeling of him stretching her, consuming her, but she wanted him wrapped around her as she fell asleep even more. As he moved in slow, luxurious strokes, she couldn't get his words out of her head. *This isn't for the baby.* It was for her. For him. For both of them.

With Drew inside her, his hands on her body and his lips kissing her neck, she finally let go of all her fears and reservations. All that was left was the here and now and each other. And the possible future that had suddenly opened up for them.

• • •

Avery practically floated through the next day, carried by the feeling of Drew kissing her awake. Even thinking back over the dinner with her family wasn't enough to dim her happiness. Last night with Drew had been so freaking perfect. After they'd made love—because there was no other term for what they'd done that seemed accurate—they'd lain in bed and watched television for hours, and then done it all over again. She was tired, but it was a good kind of tired. As she puttered around her shop, tweaking the placement of little things, she couldn't keep the goofy grin off her face.

Never in a million years would she have thought she could actually have something with Drew, and yet here she was—practically breaking out in song over him. Last night he'd said what they'd done wasn't for the baby. If it wasn't to get her pregnant, it could only be because he wanted her as much as she wanted him.

Her heart beat faster at the thought. Could this really work? They already knew they worked well on practically every level—it was impossible to be friends as long as they had and *not* work—and now they knew the sex was great, too.

Though, to be honest, it wasn't even her favorite part. She loved sneaking into her kitchen for snacks afterwards, and cuddling, and the look he kept giving her, as if he might never get enough of her. She loved it all.

She…loved him—was *in* love with him.

Avery stopped short, a fissure of fear opening inside her. This wasn't part of the plan, but… Maybe it'd be okay. He'd all but confessed feelings for her last night. He'd freaking *proposed*, even if she still couldn't take the whole marriage thing seriously. Everything between them had been different. The sex was soft and each touch had felt like he was trying to tell her something without using words, as if she was the most precious thing in the world. There was no other way to explain that without using the L word.

The bell above the shop's door rang, pulling her out of her thoughts. She rounded the giant dresser and grinned when she caught sight of Bri, carting in a car seat propped on one hip. "Hey."

"Hi." Bri held up a white bag in her free hand. "I grabbed some Diner food. I thought we could hang out. It feels like forever since I saw you last."

"I know. Things have been crazy between you and Ryan and little miss Lily, and this baby thing happening with me and Drew." And possibly even more than that.

"I always thought you two would be great together." Bri grabbed a stool and set it next to the front counter. "It's incredibly validating knowing I was right all along."

"And I always thought you were crazy."

"Thought? Past tense?"

"Things have changed since we last talked." Amazing how much could shift in a few short days, but the writing had been on the wall for them for a very long time. If she hadn't decided to have a baby, who knew if things would have escalated between them? So strange to consider that, when she felt irrevocably changed. There was no going back, not anymore. Hell, probably not from the first time they had sex.

"Things? What things? Last I heard, you were still living in the land of De Nile."

In some ways, she'd been happier there. No, that wasn't right. She was happy *now*, with Drew's words still ringing in her ears. But that didn't mean it was any less scary. "I've had a change of location since then."

Bri's blue eyes widened behind her glasses. "Holy crap, you're in love with him."

"Shhh!" She looked around, as if he'd morph out of a wall or something. Even as she did, she kicked herself for being an idiot. "It's not like that—or maybe it is. I don't know."

"Your grin is saying otherwise." Bri pushed over one of the two white bags and set Lily's car seat on the counter between them. "Here. Eat and tell me everything. I got your favorite—the bacon double cheeseburger—extra bacon."

"You're the best." Avery unwrapped the burger, her mouth watering. She moaned at the first bite. So damn good. When she finally managed to pry her eyes open, she found Bri watching her with an expectant look on her face. "Okay, fine. Yes, sometime over the last seven days, things have become more complicated."

"Good complicated?"

She laughed. "You could say that, I guess. I don't really know where his head is at with this, and it's not like I can drop the whole thing on him and tell him I love him and, oh yeah, maybe we made a baby this week. That's a lot of commitment for Drew. He'll freak out."

"You're wrong." Bri shook a bottle and popped it into Lily's mouth. "Everyone can see that Drew's been in love with you at least as long as I've known you two. Ryan claims it goes back to grade school."

"There's love and there's *love*."

"You don't have to tell me. I know. I also know that Drew *loves* you, or he wouldn't have freaked out at the thought of another man's baby in your belly." Bri sipped her soda. "You remember how you two were so sure Ryan and I were perfect for each other, no matter what we said?"

It had been a big deciding factor in their decision to strand those two. "Sure."

"This is like that."

It certainly sounded like that. She'd spent years laughing off people's questions about when she'd settle down with the older Flannery boy. What if all those people had really been onto something this entire time?

Bri smiled. "You should tell him."

Tell him and take a giant leap of faith. It might blow up in her face, but the more she thought about last night the more she was sure it wouldn't. If he weren't shifting along the same lines she'd been, he never would have said what he said. He never would have stayed over and held her while she fell asleep and then woke her up this morning with his mouth.

She took another bite, still thinking. "You might be right…"

"Yes! I most definitely am." Bri nodded at the door. "Go tell him. Lily and I will watch the shop."

"You're the best." Decision made, there was no reason to wait. She jumped to her feet and nearly ran out of the door. A feeling welled in her chest, becoming more concrete with each step she took. She loved him. Really loved him. If the last week hadn't proven just how perfect they were for each other, she didn't know what would. And hadn't all this shown that she had to grab life by both hands? It was too short to do anything else.

She'd go find him, and then she'd tell him that she wanted to keep this thing between them going. Indefinitely.

• • •

Drew's day took a turn for the shitty on his first call. "Flannery."

"Sheriff, it's Gena. We need you down at Chilly's." She made a sound freakishly close to a sob. "Rusty's in a bad way."

Goddamn it. He double-checked the time. It was barely 9 a.m. For the drunk to already be causing problems, he had to still be running strong from last night. Drew knew all too well how ugly marathons like that could get. "I'll be there in five."

"Thank you." There was a crash in the background. "Oh God, he's behind the bar."

"Gena, get out of there. I'll take care of it, okay?" The last thing he needed was for Rusty to turn on her.

All the way to Chilly's, he cursed himself for not seeing this coming. Hadn't Billy done the same damn thing time and time again? He'd work in cycles, starting with a few drinks a night—just enough to "help him sleep"—and work his way up to twenty-four hour drunk-fests where he'd inevitably end up passed out somewhere public after making an ass of himself, and then he'd be dragged home by the sheriff in front of half the town.

Rusty had been escalating and Drew *knew* it. He'd just been so busy with Avery that he'd ignored the warning signs.

He hoped like hell that no one would pay for his neglect.

He climbed out of his cruiser, able to hear Rusty's yelling from all the way out in the parking lot. Shit. He nodded at Gena, who looked scared but otherwise fine, and headed inside.

This time there was no Old Joe to stabilize the situation. There was only him and the stumbling man behind the bar. He held up a bottle of vodka when he caught sight of Drew. "Sheriff! Have a drink with me."

"Rusty, it's time to go home now." He kept his voice even and low, just like he always had with Billy, and put an easy grin on his face. "You gave Gena a hell of a scare."

"Bitch tried to take m'drink." He shook the bottle again. "I need m'drink."

It was like stepping into the past, and he wished like hell that he could just turn around and walk away from the ghost of his father standing in front of him. But Drew was sheriff now, and that meant he couldn't run. He was the one people called to deal with the messes. It was his job to clean them up.

Funny how he'd grown up but some things never changed.

He circled the end of the bar, well aware of the need to get Rusty away from the breakable bottles of liquor. "Why don't you sit down and we'll see about finding you a glass?"

"Got one." Rusty eyed him as he moved closer, now within arm's reach.

"Let's sit down." He touched the man's shoulder, guiding him out from behind the bar and into the open space between the tables. They'd barely taken three steps when Rusty shrugged him off, lurching sideways and knocking over a chair. "No. Imma not going home."

"Come on, now, don't be difficult." His patience frayed fast, driven by all the times he'd tried to reason with Billy, going through this same song and dance, with the same damn results.

"Fuck you!" Rusty swung.

Drew caught his arm and used his momentum to drive him into the bar. He hefted the man's arm behind him and pulled his cuffs in one smooth move. "You know, that shit might have worked on me as a kid, but I'm a grown ass man now."

Billy had only hit him once, but once was more than enough. Drew learned exactly how far he could push his father without eliciting *that* response, and he learned to be quicker than the alcohol-slowed reflexes.

"I lost my girls for good." The big man's body shook, with great, racking sobs. "That bitch s'took my girls away to California."

He hauled Rusty off the bar and wrestled him out of Chilly's, barely holding back the vicious words threatening. Their mother had been right to take them as far away as she could. She'd saved them from a life like Drew's had been, because men like Rusty and Billy never really changed. They only got worse with time.

Men like Drew.

And that was the problem. Billy was dead and gone. Rusty was a pain in the ass, but he wouldn't last forever at the pace he was going. No, the one he couldn't escape was himself.

He felt like a ticking time bomb, and the closer he grew to Avery, the worse it got. Because he *could* understand what it was that drove his old man to the depths of hell he'd lived in. If something ever happened to her, it was all too easy to see him repeating history.

And if there was a child in the mix?

He couldn't do that to a kid. He couldn't take that risk. Both she and the baby deserved better.

I already offered to marry her.

Right, like that was some magical solution. He'd managed to convince himself last night that marrying her would mean he wouldn't lose her, but it was a fucking lie. A hysterectomy might remove her chances of dying from the same cancer that killed her mother, but life had no guarantees. There were so many other horrible things that could go wrong.

So many other ways he could lose her.

As he drove back to the station, ignoring Rusty's slurred words in the back, he could only come to one conclusion. He had to end things with Avery. It didn't matter how good things had gotten between them. No, that was a lie, too. It was *because* things were so wonderful that he had to walk away now. If she was pregnant, then he'd hold up his end of the bargain, but he had to stop the rest.

Today.

Right now.

• • •

Avery stood as Drew stalked into his office, trying not to clasp her hands in front of her. She wasn't confessing to losing her sister's pet rabbit in the woods, or doing something wrong. This was a good thing. Good news.

Alarm bells rang in her head when he stopped and frowned at her, but she told herself she was being paranoid.

Obviously he'd just had a rough call of some sort. She gave him a tentative smile. "Hey."

"Hey." He circled wide around her, as if he didn't trust himself to get within touching distance—or didn't want to—and sat behind his desk. "What can I help you with?"

This was wrong. All kinds of wrong. He should be grinning at her and cracking a joke, not sitting there, so painfully serious that it made her chest ache. "Is everything okay?"

"Why wouldn't it be?"

That wasn't a damn answer.

She studied his face, wondering what had changed between him leaving her bed this morning and now. It was tempting to make some excuse and leave him to work through whatever his problem was, but she couldn't. She'd come here for a reason and, damn it, she was going to see it through.

So she took a deep breath and blurted it out, "I love you and I want to keep this going."

His face gave nothing away. The ache in her chest got worse because she *recognized* that look. It was the one he wore when he broke the news to his girlfriends that things were over.

Why the hell was he looking at *her* like that after what he'd said last night?

Drew stood, as if he couldn't hold himself still, but he didn't come closer. "I'm sorry, Avery."

She went still. "Sorry?" If he said it wasn't her, it was him, she was going to flip out. Hell, who was she kidding? She was half a second from flipping out right now.

"I can't do this." He rubbed a hand over his face. "Any of it. It's not in the cards for me."

"What do you mean?" She held her reaction in check because surely he wasn't saying what she thought he was saying. There was no reason to fly off the handle because—

He still wouldn't meet her gaze. "I can't be with you. You want something from me that I'm not capable of giving. I truly wish I was—maybe I even thought I was for a little bit—but I can't be what you need."

She took a step back, her body shaking as if it was going to shatter into a million jagged pieces at any moment. "You seemed more than capable of giving it to me last night." She should have known better. It had been perfect, too good to be real.

He gave her a look like she was stupid. "That was just sex. All of it was just sex. That's what we agreed on, remember?"

Their entire relationship thrown away, in a few short words. "Don't you dare. You don't get to act like I'm the one who changed the rules, when it was *you*. 'This isn't for the baby.' Remember when you said that? Because I do."

"That was a mistake." He picked up a pen and studied it. "I shouldn't have said that. You were upset. I was trying to make you feel better."

Oh God. She never would have guessed she could hurt like this, let alone that *Drew* would be the one to cause it. "You're dumping me."

"Avery, I'm not dumping you. We're friends. We'll always be friends. You were right when you said that we should go back to how things were, and I was wrong to cross that line again after we agreed not to." He sighed. "Hell, I was wrong to offer to be the sperm donor in the first place."

She started to throw something at him—mainly a fist. How could he stand there and be so unaffected while she was coming apart at the seams? No. She wouldn't give him the satisfaction of seeing her break down. She wouldn't beg him to love her, no matter how much she wanted to. "So that's it. It was all a mistake as far as you're concerned."

He finally looked at her, his blue eyes empty of any emotion. "I'll do right by you if you're pregnant. I'll hold to my end of the bargain—just like I promised."

Bargain. Such a cold word to describe what had grown between them.

But apparently *nothing* had grown between them. It had all been her, imagining something that didn't exist, desperate for whatever bones Drew would give her, and making mountains out of molehills.

She reached the door, the tornado of emotions inside her threatening to break free with every breath. "Don't bother."

"Don't be like that."

"Like what, Drew? Don't be hurt? Don't be angry? Don't walk away from you? You lost any ability to have a say thirty seconds ago when you dumped me like yesterday's trash." She threw open the door. "Don't worry about our *bargain*. I never planned on you, and I sure as fuck wouldn't be stupid enough to depend on you for a single damn thing." Not now, not with him trashing twenty years of trust in the space of two minutes. "And it's too late to go back to the way things were. Way too late."

God, her chest hurt.

He looked like he was about to say something, but she turned and walked away before he could break her heart any more than he already had. She pressed a hand to her mouth and hurried out of the police station.

As if she had anything left to break.

Chapter Eighteen

The next week passed in a blur. Drew went through the motions, but he couldn't seem to snap out of his funk. It didn't help that every day that went by made him miss Avery all the more. Normally they spent Friday nights together, but this last one had passed without a phone call from her, and he couldn't bring himself to reach out.

Too much had changed.

She wasn't just the best friend he could call and bullshit with. She was now the woman who'd said she loved him.

How the fuck was he supposed to deal with that?

The answer—he wasn't. He couldn't ask her to go back to being just friends after the way she'd shut down that option. He wasn't even sure he wanted to. All he knew was that everything had changed, and he had no idea how to navigate the new lay of the land.

It didn't help that his other friends weren't the least bit sympathetic. Bri had already shown up at his house to yell at him—something he never would have thought would happen. Even Ryan was giving him the cold shoulder. They both acted as if he'd been the biggest dick on the planet.

The worst part was he couldn't convince himself that they were wrong.

He swished the alcohol in the fifth next to him and took a swig, hating and loving the way it burned all the way down. He'd bought three bottles on his way home from work, after that horrible conversation with Avery, and he was down to his last one. He shouldn't have done it, but the hard stuff seemed apt. And it was the only thing that could chase the memories away long enough to let him get some sleep.

Like father, like son.

He glanced up as his front door opened, and flinched when he caught sight of his brother standing there. Ryan took a long look around the living room, and Drew followed his gaze, hating what he saw—old pizza boxes, empty bottles, and Drew himself, wearing the same clothes he had for the last two days. He wanted to yell at his brother, to wave his hand around at the mess that was all too familiar from their childhood and obvious proof that he was right all along— he'd lost the person he cared about most in the world and now he was circling the drain—but he couldn't work up the energy even for that. "Have you come to kick my ass?"

"No." Ryan crossed his arms over his chest. "You look like shit."

He raised the bottle. "We all deal with things in our own way."

"So your way is to drink yourself into a coma? Since when do you touch that shit?" He nodded at the vodka. The same brand Billy used to drink.

"Since last Tuesday."

"So you're just going to sit here and have a pity party until you're vying with Rusty for Town Drunk status. Sounds like a solid life plan."

Drew struggled to get off the couch. "You don't get to judge me."

"Wrong. I get to do whatever I damn well have to in order to snap you out of this shit." Ryan marched over and snatched the bottle out of his hand. Before he could react, his brother was gone, the sound of liquid swishing down the sink quickly following.

"Hey!"

Ryan reappeared in the doorway. "I can't stop you from going out and buying another, but I'm telling you right now, I'll be here every single fucking day to pour them out as fast as you can bring them in." He shook his head. "I was too young to do a damn thing about our dad, but I sure as fuck am not watching you walk down the same path."

"You think I *want* this? I don't. I never wanted to be him. But obviously it's in me or I wouldn't be here." He hit his chest.

"That's an excuse, and not even a good one at that. You fucked things up with Avery, and now you're punishing yourself." He grabbed Drew's phone from the coffee table and shoved it at him. "Call her. Fix it."

"It's not that simple." He wished it were. "It would never work with her."

"Why? No, wait. Let me ask you a question first."

He really didn't want to know what the question was. "Fine."

"Why did you offer to do this to begin with? And don't

give me that shit about being a good friend. I'm a good friend to Avery, and it never would have occurred to me to offer to be her sperm donor, let alone the shit you put forward. So why did you? Was it just curiosity? Did you just want to know what it was like to sleep with her?"

"*No.*" The thought that his brother assumed he'd slept with Avery out of sheer curiosity made him sick to his stomach. "I would never screw with her like that."

"Really? Because I'm pretty sure you've done exactly that. Not to mention, I know for a fact you've been careful to a paranoid degree to avoid being a dad. So *why?*"

Why? Because the thought of her having another man's baby made him crazy. Even after finding out it would have literally been a sperm donor, he couldn't deal with the idea of sitting by and watching her stomach swell with a stranger's kid.

That…wasn't a normal response.

"I…" Drew took a deep breath and really *looked* at his motivations like he hadn't dared do since he'd told her it was over. Deep down, had he really wanted *his* child inside her?

Yes.

Shit.

Ryan snorted. "'I?' Is that the best you got? That isn't a legit reason."

He always knew he cared about Avery—loved her, even—but that possessive feeling had only shown up once she decided to get pregnant. And his need for her…that wasn't manufactured, or expected. Still, he dug in his heels. Maybe he wanted her as more than friend, but that didn't mean all his fears were unfounded. "I don't want to lose my best friend."

For the first time since Ryan walked through the door, some sympathy slid into his voice. "Who said you have to have one or the other? These things aren't mutually exclusive."

"But things worked so perfectly before. We've fought more in the last week than we did in the two years before that."

"Maybe because you finally found something you wanted enough to fight for. Jesus, Drew, you know your relationship with Avery wasn't static, right? Eventually she was going to find a guy, and then it'd change anyways."

"I don't want to lose her," he repeated. He motioned at the destruction of his living room. "You want proof why? This is more than enough proof. What if it doesn't work out? What if something happens to her? It'll be our old man all over again. I can't do that to some innocent kid."

Some of the anger left Ryan's face. "You actually think you'd do what he did?"

"Look around you. I already have."

"Only because you're so determined to prove you're right that you're doing it to yourself."

Had he created his own self-fulfilling prophecy? The sick feeling in his stomach only got worse when his brother voiced the very thing he'd been going out of his way not to think about for the last week. "I can't be a father. Not with everything."

"Hey, idiot, I just got married and had a baby. I grew up the same as you did."

No, he hadn't. Which was the entire point. "Bullshit. I practically raised you. I made sure you never went without."

Ryan met his gaze, his blue eyes unflinching. "Yeah, you

did."

He stopped short. *Yeah, he had.* He'd never thought about it like that before. When he was a kid, he was so focused on getting from point A to point B, and providing for his little brother. Once he was an adult, he'd done everything in his power to look forward—never back. "Ryan—"

"As much as I'd like to sit here and listen to you try to justify letting Avery go, I actually have better things to do with my day. Figure out what you want. That's all I've got right now." He stopped just inside the door. "By the way, Avery is pregnant. Bri camped out with seven pregnancy tests yesterday while she drank her weight in water."

Bri had held her hand while she waited for the news. Not Drew. He should have been there for her, not drinking himself into oblivion. He hated that he'd missed out on the look on her face when she saw the test results. "Why didn't she call me?"

"You know why." Then Ryan was gone, closing the door softly behind him.

He'd missed this. If he kept going down this path, he'd miss *everything*. He wouldn't be there to help her through morning sickness, or to run to the store for whatever she was craving, or to see her grow big with his child. He wouldn't be there for her to scream at in the delivery room, or to count the baby's fingers and toes.

Was he really going to let his fear stand in the way of watching his kid grow from a baby to a little person to an adult? Was he willing to miss out on a lifetime with Avery?

No. Fuck no. He wanted to be there, and not just as a favorite uncle. He wanted to be *there*. To be in her bed and in her life and with her through the good, the bad, and the ugly.

He wanted it all.

But this time he wanted it all for the right reasons.

He ran his hands through his hair as he paced through his living room. There had to be a way to make this right. Even as the thought crossed his mind, he stopped. What did he have to offer her? He couldn't go in with some weak shit about seeing where things went. She'd tell him to go to hell—and rightfully so. If he wanted Avery in his life, he was going to have to prove he was in this for the long haul.

But how…

He grabbed his phone and dialed. Bri picked up and, before she could lay into him again, he cut in. "I know I screwed up majorly and I'm sorry. I swear to God, you have no idea how sorry I am. I'm going to make it right, but I need your help with something."

The pause stretched on so long, he was worried she'd hung up. Finally, she sighed. "I'm listening."

So Drew took a deep breath and outlined his plan. It was his Hail Mary pass and he damn well knew it. After the way he dropped the ball with Avery, there was no guaranteeing that even this would be enough. But he had to try. If he didn't, he'd spend the rest of his life regretting letting her go without a fight.

He just hoped it wasn't already too late.

• • •

Avery sat in the waiting room and did her damnedest not to cry. It wouldn't do a damn bit of good, but her tear ducts apparently hadn't gotten the memo. She wished she could blame her mood on hormones alone, but it would be a dirty lie. The truth was, she felt as if she'd lost half her heart. Every move hurt, until all she wanted to do was curl up in bed and wait for the pain to pass.

But that would be giving up.

She'd picked this path knowing it might blow up in her face. She shouldn't be surprised that it had. Hell, she should have been expecting it. She knew Drew's history. She'd lived through it, watching him escape from every single relationship he'd ever been in.

It had just never occurred to her that he'd escape *theirs*.

And, worse, she'd fallen for him hook, line, and sinker. Instead of listening to what he was saying, she'd been reading into everything he'd done. If she couldn't handle them having sex, she never should have agreed to this in the first place.

She was the worst kind of idiot. She'd just lost her best friend and what could be the love of her life, all because she'd grabbed too much and expected him to change. He didn't love her—not as more than a friend, anyways.

She bent over, trying to breathe through the pain in her chest at the thought. He'd been doing her a favor. All of it— the sex, the touching, the cuddling—it had all been because she wanted to get pregnant. Not because he really wanted her. She'd just wanted him so desperately, she'd somehow managed to convince herself that he wanted her that way, too.

It was too late to go back and demand a do-over. She was in this alone. Avery pressed her hand to her stomach and corrected herself—not alone. She'd never be alone again. It should have made her deliriously happy. This was what she wanted. And she *was* happy, but it was hard to get excited when her heart was breaking into a thousand tiny pieces.

God, she was such a cliché.

"Avery."

Bracing herself, she got to her feet and followed the nurse back to the room. Unsurprisingly, she'd actually lost weight in the last week—hard to work up an appetite with a broken heart. At least everything else seemed to be normal.

With one last reassuring smile, the nurse closed the door behind her, leaving Avery to stew alone. And, as it always did when she stopped moving for half a second, her traitorous mind circled back to the look on Drew's face when she told him she loved him. The perfectly blank expression.

She *was* the one who'd gone and changed the rules. He'd always held up to his end of the "bargain." Technically, she didn't have any justifiable reason for being angry at him.

That didn't stop her from wanting to drive to his house, kick down his door, and smack some sense into him. If she didn't know how much it *wouldn't* work, she might have already tried it. But no one could convince Drew to change his mind except Drew. If she tried, she'd just number herself among the broken hearts he left in a trail behind him.

Avery shook her head. What the hell was she thinking? Letting Drew go without a fight? The only thing that would save was her pride and, goddamn it, her pride wouldn't keep her warm at night. Drew had said that he wanted things to work between them, that he wanted *her*. He might be flighty as hell when it came to dating, but he'd never been a liar.

Screw being the bigger man. She was going to track him down and give that asshole a piece of her mind.

. . .

By the time Avery made it home, she was dead on her feet. Drew wasn't at work or his house or Chilly's. He had apparently dropped off the face of the earth. She could have kept searching, but exhaustion set in after the third place she'd looked.

When everyone talked about pregnancy, all they focused on was the glow and how wonderful it was feeling a new life grow inside you. No one mentioned the near-constant need for naps.

One hour. One hour of sleep and then she'd get up and hit the grocery store for food. The doctor said she was healthy, but she needed to make sure she was getting enough nutrients for the baby.

She unlocked her front door and froze at the sight that greeted her. Someone had transformed her living room into… There were no words. It looked like a baby store had vomited all over her place. There were pink and blue baby things covering every inch of available space, including two cribs, two strollers, two changing tables…

What the hell?

Drew stepped out of the kitchen and, for the first time in as long as she could remember, he looked hesitant. As if he wasn't sure of his welcome. There were also massive dark circles beneath his eyes, and he'd lost at least as much weight as she had. Put shortly, he looked like shit.

"Hey."

Hey? That's the best he could come up with? She crossed her arms over her chest, fighting against the need to run across the room and throw herself at him and beg him to love her. She was better than that. She *deserved* better than that. "Hi."

"I'm an asshole." He shoved his hands through his hair, making the curls stick out at odd angles. "I am so goddamn sorry that I said that shit in my office. I was wrong, and this time, I really mean it. It was a dick move and you deserve better than that."

Never in a million years would she have guessed that he'd show up in her house like the freaking Baby Gift Fairy and apologize. But then he kept talking, and it was like the entire world stood still.

"The truth is, I was scared shitless. I was just coming to terms with that fact that I'm in love with your crazy ass, when suddenly I'm understanding *exactly* what pushed my dad over the edge—because I can see myself going the same route if I lost you." His eyes looked so bleak that, against all reason, she wanted to hug him. "Loving someone so much and losing them—I can't even blame him for losing his shit anymore."

"Hold on. Rewind and say that again."

He frowned. "I'm an asshole?"

"Yeah, I got that part. The other thing." And they were most definitely addressing his view of his father the first chance she got.

His expression cleared. "I love you, Avery. God, I love you so much it still scares me. I almost let you slip through my fingers because I was terrified, and I love you and, Jesus, can you ever forgive me?"

Could she?

Avery knew the answer before she finished the thought. *Yes.* But still she held back. This was more than her life now. This was her baby's, too. "Are you sure? This is a big commitment, Drew. Loving—" Her voice caught, but she powered on. "Loving me isn't enough."

"Love is everything." He took one slow step toward her, and then another. "Love is what got us into this situation, and love is going to be what keeps us going through sleepless nights, and potty training, and the dreaded teenage years. Love and the kind of crazy only you and I can bring to a situation." He finally stood in front of her and reached for her hand. "And love is what had me dragging Bri to Babies 'R' Us and listening to her lectures on how I don't actually need two of everything."

She looked around the room again, finally starting to register just how much stuff he'd bought. "Why *did* you buy two of everything?"

"While it was pointedly declared to me that one of everything in green or yellow would be fine, I wanted us to have the right color when we found out if our baby is a boy or girl." His grin rocked her right down to her soul. "So I got two of everything."

"Drew…" All of her arguments about why this might not work were disappearing right under her feet. Because she *wanted* this to work. She wanted it so bad, she could taste it.

Which scared the crap out of her. "I can't go through that again. I can't get into this only to have you decide you can't handle it."

"I thought you might say that." And then the bastard got down on one knee. While she stared, trying to think past the rushing in her ears, he pulled out a little square box and opened it. "Avery Yeung, I've loved you since that day in first grade when you punched me in the face, and that love has only grown over the years, through all the crazy shit we've gotten into. I was an idiot not to face up to it before, but I'm hoping I can make up for lost time starting now. Will you marry me?"

When she only stared, he rushed on. "I saw this down at one of those antique shops in Williamsport you love so much and it practically screamed your name. The owner said it was once owned by some oil tycoon's mistress. I figured it was time to make an honest diamond of it."

"You're serious." She couldn't seem to connect reality with fantasy. Never in a million years would she have guessed Drew would come back, let alone come back like *this*.

"As a heart attack. I fucked up. Really fucked up. And, I swear to God, I'm going to spend the rest of our lives making it up to you."

"You went to a baby store for me."

"Also, the ring." He shook the box. "Let's not forget the ring."

"You bought me two of everything."

"Again, the ring."

Avery finally let free the smile that had been bubbling up inside her as soon as he told her he loved her. "You really don't do anything halfway, do you?"

"Avery…"

Could a person die of happiness? She might actually be in danger of that. Avery threw her arms around Drew, toppling them to the floor. She kissed him once, twice, three times. "Yes. Of course I'll marry you and love you forever and drive you out of your mind with my mad schemes."

His grin nearly stopped her heart as he slipped the ring on her finger. "I figured maybe we could wait until the baby's a year old and then start looking into adopting," he said.

"Kid's going to need a sibling or two."

And there went her ovaries. "I love you so goddamn much."

"That's good, because I'd hate to have to lock you in my basement to be my love slave for the rest of your life," he said, his grin fading to mock sternness. "As I am a respected member of this community, the rest of the Sheriff's department might frown upon something like that."

She nodded, fighting to keep a straight face. "I'm glad I could save you from having to go to such extreme lengths."

"It's very noble of you."

Avery laughed. "You're ridiculous. Now shut up and kiss me—then tell me you love me again."

"I love you, I love you, I love you. And I'm going to spend the next fifty years telling you that every damn day."

Epilogue

"My water broke!"

Avery rolled her eyes at Drew. "You are way too into this game." The baby chose that moment to kick and she pressed her hand to her stomach. The last few months had been surreal in the best way possible, and Drew had been by her side every step of the way, through the morning sickness and every single doctor's appointment and her weird ass craving for butter smeared on saltines.

He held up his glass of Sprite. Sure enough the tiny baby that had previously been encased in ice was now floating free. Drew raised his voice. "Bri, did you hear? My water broke. Pretty sure that means I win."

Bri sailed over, Lily propped on one hip. "Looks like it! Just a second." Then she was gone. She'd been super peppy ever since they showed up for the baby shower an hour ago. Hell, she'd been excessively energetic since she'd offered to throw it for Avery a couple of weeks earlier. Avery had considered asking Alexis, but she didn't know if that would hurt more than it would help, so she'd let Bri take the reins. Apparently her friend had decided to run with it…and then some.

She looked around. Chilly's had been transformed, blue and pink banners everywhere, and all the tables covered with equally jarring tableclothes. They'd decided not to find out if the baby was a boy or girl, so the theme was less a theme than an explosion of all things baby.

She loved it.

She wandered over to grab more carrots from the veggie tray, then stopped next to her father. "Hey, Dad." Things hadn't smoothed out with her grandparents, but he'd been there, offering his quiet and unconditional support.

"How's the little pea pod doing?"

"Oh, you know, baby kept me up all night rolling around. I swear this kid is an octopus and not a human."

"Your mom said the same thing when she was pregnant with you." A shadow passed over his face, but cleared almost immediately. "I wish she was here to see this."

"Me, too." She'd been spending a lot of time thinking about her mom lately. Dad had found her and Alexis's old baby books, and reading them had been bittersweet. Their mother's love came through the pages in technicolor, her bubbly handwriting filled with joy and excitement about her pregnancies and new babies. Avery couldn't help but think she would have made a wonderful grandmother.

Oh great, now I'm going to cry again. Goddamn hormones.

She wiped her eyes, needing to change the subject to something safer. "Have you seen Alexis?" Her sister had said she'd be there, but Avery hadn't heard from her yet.

"No." He frowned. "I thought she'd have shown up by now."

Her sister wasn't late. Ever. "Maybe she texted me and I missed it."

Avery hurried back to her table. She didn't make it to her phone before Drew hooked her around her hips and towed her into his lap. "Hey, sexy."

"There is nothing sexy about—what did your daddy baby book call me?—a hippo or a whale." She grinned. "But you can show your appreciation with a foot rub later if you want. My ankles are killing me."

"Your wish is my command." He kissed her. "Sit for a bit. You've been running around almost as much as Bri. The doctor said to take it easy."

"No, the doctor said that if I felt like I was overdoing it, I should prop my feet up and take it easy." She patted her belly. "We have two months to go, and a whole hell of a lot to do before then."

"Avery."

She knew that tone of voice. It was one he'd developed ever since he'd more or less moved into her house. Drew had been worried that she'd somehow magically hurt herself and be unable to reach the phone if she was in the middle of nowhere at his place, so the plan was to be at her house during her pregnancy and the first six months, and then move to his after the wedding. He'd gone so far as to bring home one of those life alert buttons that elderly people wore around their neck—which was where she drew the line. She wasn't an invalid.

She crossed her arms over her chest. "I'm fine." When he just pinned her with a hard look, she snarled. "If I promise to take a damn nap after the baby shower, will you get off my case?"

Drew grinned. "Deal."

He'd played her and she damn well knew it, but she couldn't bring herself to be more than a little annoyed. It wasn't a bad thing that he cared so much, and there was a certain level of comfort that came from his overprotective pestering. "You're insufferable."

"You love it. That's why you put a ring on it."

She eyed the ring she'd bought him a few months ago—the ring he'd refused to take off, despite the fact it was against tradition to wear it before the wedding. "Yeah, well, you're pretty awesome, and I'm kind of totally head over heels in love with you."

"Good answer." He kissed her, a quick brush of his lips against hers. It was the kind of casually intimate touch that they couldn't seem to be in the same room without doing. At first, it had weirded her out a little, but now it anchored her, a tiny reminder that this was real. This man. This life. This future. All of it was really happening.

"Here's your prize, Drew." Bri set a wrapped present on the table. "Everyone, it's time for the next game!"

"You've created a monster," he whispered in her ear.

"Shut up. She's having fun. We're having fun. It's all good."

Avery allowed herself to be swept up into the barely controlled chaos of her friends and family. She was so busy, she forgot about trying to contact her sister until nearly an hour later.

"Crap!"

Instantly, Drew was at her side. "What is it? Is it the

baby? Do we have to go to the hospital?"

"What? No. The baby is fine—wedged under my ribs and all up in my lungs, but fine." She hurried around him and snatched her phone off the table where she'd left it. Sure enough, there was a text waiting.

I wanted to be there today. Really, I did. I love you and I support you and am genuinely happy for you, but it hurts. God, it hurts, Avery. But that's MY problem, and something that I have to deal with on my own. It will be okay, but I've got to go away for a bit. I'll be back before my niece or nephew is born, though. I promise!

Avery reread the text twice and handed it to Drew. "Alexis left."

"What?" He frowned as he read. "Where?"

"I don't know."

He turned for the door. "We've got to find her."

"Wait." She grabbed his arm. A part of her wanted to chase Alexis down, but it was the selfish part of her. Her sister had been dancing to everyone else's tune for too long. If she needed to escape for a little while, she was entitled to it. She slid into Drew's arms. "We'll figure it out tomorrow." Which would give her sister plenty of time to get where she was going. "Right now, we're having a baby shower for our baby. You wouldn't want to drag me out of here and deprive me of that cake I've been jonesing for, would you?"

Drew smiled, though there was still worry lingering in his eyes. "God forbid." He smoothed back her hair. "We're making a baby."

"*I'm* making a baby. You made five percent of a baby."

It was becoming an old joke between them and, sure enough, he laughed. "It was a good five percent."

"The best." She went up onto her tiptoes and kissed him. "I love you like whoa. Have I mentioned that today?"

"I never get tired of hearing it." He glanced around. "What do you say we get out of here and go for a drive?"

"A drive?" What the hell was he talking about?

"Yeah, back to our place—and our bed."

Avery burst out laughing. "Oh, hell no. We can get down and dirty later. Right now, cake trumps hot and sweaty sex." Though the acrobatics were on hold while she was roughly the size of a barge, they were still damn near insatiable for each other.

"You wound me."

"You'll live." She still couldn't quite belive that this was her life. She had Drew, and a baby on the way, and everything was as perfect as an imperfect thing like life could be. She grabbed his hand and towed him toward the dessert table. "Come on, Romeo, let's feed this baby."

Acknowledgments

To God. This year has been filled with more good than bad, and for that I can't thank you enough.

To Heather Howland. For helping me get this book into fighting shape.

To Kari Olson. For being a fan of Drew way back when!

To Jen McLaughlin. For betaing this book and loving Drew as much as I do!

To Trent, PJ, and Seleste, for you're continuing support and always being willing to let me bounce ideas off you.

To my family. Another one bites the dust! Dinner's on me tonight!

To my readers. Thank you so much for your unrelenting excitement and patience waiting for Drew and Avery's story. I hope you love their story as much as I do!

About the Author

New York Times and USA Today bestselling author, Katee Robert, learned to tell stories at her grandpa's knee. Her favorites then were the rather epic adventures of The Three Bears, but at age twelve she discovered romance novels and never looked back. Though she dabbled in writing, life got in the way, as it often does, and she spent a few years traveling, living in both Philadelphia and Germany. In between traveling and raising her two wee ones, she had the crazy idea that she'd like to write a book and try to get published.

.

Betting on Fate

Protecting Fate

Seducing the Bridesmaid

Meeting His Match

Sanctify series

The High Priestess

Queen of Swords

Queen of Wands

CPSIA information can be obtained
at www.ICGtesting.com
Printed in the USA
LVHW021520100119
603456LV00001B/40/P